COSEGA SEARCH

Book One of the Cosega Sequence

BRANDT LEGG

LAUGHING RAIN

Cosega Search (Book One of the Cosega Sequence)

Published in the United States of America by Laughing Rain

Copyright © 2014 by Brandt Legg
    All rights reserved.

Cataloging-in-Publication data for this book is available from
the Library of Congress.
    ISBN-13: 978-1-935070-07-8
    ISBN-10: 1-935070-07-X

Cover designed by: Eleni Karoumpali

PUBLISHER'S NOTE
    This book is a work of fiction. Names, characters, places, and
incidents are products of the author's imagination or are used
fictitiously. Any resemblance to actual persons, living or dead,
businesses, events, or locales is entirely coincidental.

This book is dedicated to Teakki and Ro

1

Monday July 10th

"How quickly can you get to Virginia?" Larsen Fretwell's voice boomed through the satphone.

"I'm in the middle of nowhere, Idaho on day seventeen of a dig," Ripley "Rip" Gaines replied, wiping away dust and sweat as he switched to his other ear. "What do you have?"

He didn't want to leave yet. As usual, his sponsors thought the famed archaeologist was looking for one thing, but his hopes were elsewhere. A few early artifacts made him optimistic about this site, even though he'd been disappointed at seven previous locations.

"It's a Cosega find. Get here now!"

Larsen, a former student, trusted colleague, and his closest friend, knew the parameters. If he'd discovered a piece of Cosega then everything would change; the early history of the human race and all in the world that had come after.

After a long flight, the Virginia humidity greeted him. He'd been picked up at Dulles International Airport outside Washington, D.C. by a "kid" about twenty-five years old who didn't seem to know much about the discovery, or at least who wasn't willing to say.

The heavy, humid air reminded Rip of countless digs in the tropics. It made him comfortable, like the embrace of an old friend. The ancient Blue Ridge Mountains always felt welcoming, yet mysterious at the same time. He had spent most of his summers growing up in these mountains just a few hundred miles south. Their Jeep turned up a steep, rutted dirt road on the edge of the unending Jefferson National Forest.

Rip ran a hand through his dusty brown hair and tried to imagine what Larsen had found. Larsen's words *"a Cosega find"* had been playing over in his mind almost constantly since he'd heard them. Cosega was the reason that Rip became an archaeologist. The Jeep's motor whined as it pushed over the unmaintained road.

Rip's thoughts drifted to the past. They always did when he was in the mountains. Fifteen years earlier he had graduated from the University of Pennsylvania with honors after publishing a series of papers on the prehistory of man. His first break came when billionaire Booker Lipton, a Penn alumnus who had amassed a fortune through brutal corporate takeovers and a variety of other business dealings, immediately offered him funding.

Rip had skipped the "cap and gown nonsense," as he called it, and was already in Africa when his degree caught up with him. His first human origins digs were featured in an eight-page layout for *National Geographic*. Within a few years *Archaeology Magazine* had twice detailed his findings for cover stories. He taught courses at three different universities, and often shared his expertise on news and talk shows. Then, four years ago, he published a paper on the creation stories of all known Native American tribes entitled: *Cosega*. The controversy that erupted after had almost ended his career. Not yet forty, Ripley had already achieved more than the greats in his field who were twice his age. All this had left the hazel-eyed, ruggedly handsome professor with an empty social life, but his single-minded pursuit of the past allowed little room for dating.

"Dr. Gaines, I just want you to know that you're the reason I decided to become an archaeologist," his young driver said.

"Don't blame that on me," Rip answered, only half joking.

"When I read your Cosega Theory, I switched my major from geology," he said. "It just makes sense. More than Clovis or Cactus Hill."

Rip nodded, not in the mood to talk. It had been impossible to concentrate on anything other than the sketchy details Larsen had dangled, but the kid deserved some kind of response from his academic hero.

"You know Cosega is still a dangerous word in most scientific circles. A lot of people think I'm crazy."

"They said the same thing about Galileo."

"Ah, but I'm no Galileo."

"People used to think that 15,000 years ago humans walked out of Africa, and a few thousand years later they made it to a land bridge over the Bering Strait and into Alaska. And the finds in Clovis, New Mexico seemed to back that theory up. Alaska," the driver continued. "Prior to that it was thought that the Americas were devoid of any human presence."

Rip knew all this of course, but as long as they were getting closer to Larsen and his discovery he'd just let the kid talk.

"But then the Cactus Hill, Virginia site proved that people had been here at least 20,000 years."

"Allegedly," Rip corrected. "There is some controversy surrounding Cactus Hill." He laughed. "And I'm an expert on controversy."

"Yeah, well all that is dependent on the thesis that modern humans evolved between 50,000 and 100,000 years ago. Your Cosega Theory disputes it all."

"Yes, it does," Rip said. "But it is only the ramblings of a mad man unless I can find something that proves that humans have been around for hundreds of thousands of years."

"Dr. Fretwell might just have found your proof."

2

The Jeep finally entered the research area and wove through eleven tents and several parked trucks before halting on the edge of a thicket of trees. The intoxicating scent of pine and honeysuckle enveloped him. Larsen, his former student, met them along the path and Rip braced for the bear hug. Rip stood just over six feet tall, but he appeared small next to the six-foot-seven Larsen, whose massive arms wrapped around him and lifted him off the ground.

"This time we have something," Larsen said, laughing. Known for his almost freakishly large hands, he opened his right fist, revealing an artifact. "I call it the 'Odeon' because it reminds me of the ancient Greek theatre."

Ripley Gaines had read every archaeology paper that mattered, reviewed countless photos, and had taken part in digs on every continent. He always said, *"There's nothing new in the past."* Yet here he was, gazing at something he could never have conjured even in his most radical theories.

It shimmered like expensive pearls, a flat, near perfect oval the size of a bar of soap made from an almost transparent quartz-like substance. Three evenly spaced inlaid gold lines –

about an eighth of an inch thick — circled the narrow circumference.

"Incredible!" Rip's adrenaline was pumping. "What level are you at?"

"It's old." His expression turned serious. "It's too old."

"Beyond Cosega?"

"A thousand times beyond."

Rip looked at Larsen. He clutched the proof of Cosega tightly in his hand. "Take me to the origin point."

"There's something else," Larsen said. "After I called you, we made a more significant discovery."

Rip stared at the Odeon he held. "More than this?"

Larsen nodded. "We're close to extracting it."

Rip impatiently pushed past Larsen. He could see the dig up ahead at the bottom of a twenty-foot limestone cliff. Larsen caught up as Rip reached four graduate students, working the tedious details. Ten or twelve other students stood watching, one shooting photos, but Rip didn't notice any of them. He knew that the cliff had to be millions of years old. If the Odeon did come from there, then the Cosega Theory, minus a major mathematical error, would now be the "Cosega Rule."

"Dr. Fretwell!" one of the students shouted to Larsen. "We're about to cut the last section away."

Larsen nodded. "Do it."

A few minutes later, the students stepped back while Rip peered inside the shaft, which had been carefully cut into the cliff.

"Cosega," Larsen whispered behind him.

With trembling hands, Rip tried to comprehend the sight. Sweat burned his eyes that refused to blink. *It's the world's past, and my future,* he thought. Then, turning to Larsen and pointing toward the object still resting within its stone hiding place, Rip said, "Do you see it, Larsen? You're looking inside the change."

Rip remained mesmerized by the intricately carved stone globe that he'd just pulled out of the cliff until a woman asked over his shoulder, "Isn't that cliff millions of years old? How could something perfectly round, with those carvings, come out of there?"

Rip spun around startled and scowled. A digital recorder was pushed toward his face.

"Dr. Gaines. Have you finally found proof of your Cosega Theory?" she asked.

"Who the hell are you?" he demanded.

"I'm eight million readers worldwide who want to know what you found up here."

"Jesus Christ! You're with the media? What is she doing here?" He turned to Larsen, shouting, "Get her out of here!"

The man with a camera began shooting. Rip instinctively moved away, trying to shield the artifact.

"Damn it, Larsen. How did the freaking media get in?"

"They're not technically here as media," Larsen stuttered. "I mean... sort of."

"I don't care who they are. Why is he shooting this?" Rip motioned wildly. "Get them out!"

"Josh is an old friend. I wanted independent verification of the find. He lives a few hours away in Fredericksburg."

"Gale Asher." The woman held out her hand. "A pleasure to meet you, Dr. Gaines. I'm with *National Geographic* and—"

"Are you kidding me!?" Rip yelled at Larsen, completely ignoring Gale.

Gale smiled. Rip's gruffness neither surprised nor intimidated her. She knew the media had been increasingly rough on him the past few years since he first published his theory.

"I need you both to leave." He felt sick as his arm motioned from Gale to Josh. "And I'll need the memory card from your camera. This is a privately funded dig."

"You're on federal land, and besides, we were invited," Gale challenged.

Rip glared at Larsen. "Well, consider yourself uninvited. It's a matter of safeguarding the dig from contamination, scientific protocols, protection of antiquities, and site security."

Her curly blonde hair escaped from a small blue ball cap in a futile attempt at a ponytail. Somehow that wild mane made Gale seem even more dangerous to Rip, and she was not as gullible as he would have liked. As a reporter with the Wall Street Journal for six years, she'd regularly heard lies from corrupt politicians and executives. Finally, fed up with the hypocrisy and greed of the business world, she took a position with *National Geographic*, drawn by the chance to cover the planet's beauty rather than the worst of its inhabitants.

Stepping toward him, she fired off a series of wide-ranging questions about the dig and his career, then with alarming accuracy recounted the results of almost every excavation he had done. Her preparation and knowledge both impressed and annoyed him.

"Screw this. You three," Rip shouted to three students in the crowd, "get tarps and screen off this entire area. No one goes in without my approval."

The students looked at Larsen.

"Do it now!" Rip yelled.

Larsen nodded his approval at the students.

Rip scooped up someone's parka lying next to a box of bottled water and trail bars and wrapped it around the globe.

"You there," he said to a guy working a sifter. "I want you to hold your screen to block any shots this clown tries to take until the tarps are up. Get in his face. Be rude if necessary. He's only a member of the media."

"Rip, you're being a little heavy-handed," Larsen said.

"And a bit overly dramatic," Gale added.

"Am I?" He looked at Larsen. "Did you see this thing? Think of the level, Larsen . . . think of the goddamn level and tell me I'm overreacting. What was going through your head when you let them in before we even got it out?"

"Whose dig is this?" Gale asked.

Rip, ignoring her, headed down the trail toward the camp.

Gale's long, blonde curls whipped around as she turned to yell after him. Her ten-pocket, tan safari shorts and dusty white cotton blouse made her appear like one of the grad students. "You can't stop this story, Dr. Gaines. It's too late. The past doesn't belong to you!"

3

Alone inside a tent, Rip peeled away the parka slowly, like someone unwrapping a prized birthday present. Slightly bigger than a basketball and with its strange carvings, the globe didn't belong in a prehistoric archaeological site. Gale's question amplified in his head. *"How could a smooth round stone, carved by man, be embedded in eleven-million-year-old rock?"*

All of recorded history had just been blown apart. Even his insane Cosega Theory was inadequate against this thing.

Larsen found him. "Rip, I'm sorry about Gale and Josh. But this was going to get out. And Josh is an old friend. We'll have more control with them."

"Look at this, Larsen. Tell me. How is this millions of years old?"

"It's the object of your obsession," Larsen said. "More than you imagined, isn't it?"

Rip studied the carvings, cut about a quarter of an inch into the dark grey stone. "These inlaid gold bands, just like on the Odeon, come out from the equator. But it's the etched circles that are most promising. They aren't random. Do you see the pattern?" Rows of circles within circles, interrupted by lines of two different lengths and other "columns" of dashes filled the surface of the globe. "Do you think it's some kind of binary language?"

Larsen raised an eyebrow. "It's way too old for anything like that. Let's get it to my tent. I've got a kit there. We need to weigh and measure it." Larsen's tent was roomier and included a table and chairs.

Rip sat holding the globe. "Catch me up on how we got here. Start with the Odeon," he said, not taking his eyes off the treasure.

"As you know, we started at the human-formed wall," Larsen began.

The site, covering an area the size of two football fields, had been accidentally discovered more than a year before when two National Forest employees stumbled upon a three-thousand-year-old stone foundation. Rip, always watching for finds that don't quite fit the standard history, obtained funding from Booker and asked Larsen to take a look. They began excavating the site three months ago and had found several layers of artifacts, some going back eight or nine thousand years. The area had been inhabited for centuries prior to the arrival of Europeans. Its reliable water sources, plentiful game, along with the protection of the surrounding cliffs, had made it an ideal area for settlements over the ages. As they dug through the levels, multiple traces of human activity were discovered.

"It's been typical for months," Larsen continued. "A rich but routine dig until a couple of days ago. While clearing underbrush to expand the perimeters, one of the guys noticed the smooth edge of what turned out to be the Odeon sticking out of the cliff. The gold bands glinting in the sun caught his eye. I called you as soon as we got it out."

"It's not connected to the rest of the site?" Rip asked rhetorically.

"The cliff, as you know, is limestone. The recent heavy spring runoff finally eroded enough of it away to expose the Odeon."

"And the globe?"

"My team was meticulous. I had them in there with dental picks. Once we freed the Odeon, they poked through to a larger cavity behind. The globe was just sitting in there."

"Was the cavity natural or carved?"

"Inconclusive." He pulled out a scale. Rip reluctantly handed him the globe. "It's surprisingly light," Larsen said. "Four point three kilos, about nine and a half pounds."

"I thought the same thing. It should be heavier." Rip took it off the scale.

"Without testing we can't be sure, but I have to believe this object is millions of years old." Larsen looked at Rip, a dire expression on his face. "There is no other explanation, but . . . it's not possible."

"Cosega says it is."

"But not like this. Not this old."

"How do we know? The past is hiding four point five billion years of secrets. We're not even in kindergarten."

"Then you believe?"

"I believe this thing is older than man, of unknown origin, and we just pulled it out of a Virginia cliff," he said in a hushed tone. "All of my training and experience are useless at this moment." They studied it until finally Rip got up and opened the tent flaps. "We need more light." He moved it gently from hand to hand.

"It's beautiful," Larsen said. "And you're right. Those gold bands are identical to the ones on the Odeon."

Rip had not taken the Odeon out of his pocket since they discovered the globe.

"Let's compare them," he said. While moving the globe into his left hand, his thumbs moved along the top and bottom of the globe. It separated.

"It's hollow! Larsen, do you believe this? It's *hollow!*"

Before Larsen could move to get a good look, a glassy, black, inner sphere rolled out of the stone globe, which now appeared to be more of a casing to protect the true prize in Rip's lap.

"My God," Larsen whispered.

Rip carefully placed the stone casings on the table. They looked like two matching ancient bowls now.

"This is almost frightening," he said, blinking disbelievingly at the black inner sphere. As he turned it slowly in his hands, the polished surface reflected the tent's interior.

"We've got to document it," Larsen said.

"If word gets out, the media, thieves, and souvenir hunters will converge on this place. We need time."

"We *need* to document it," Larsen repeated.

"Tell me about this photographer?"

"He's a friend – a good guy."

"I guess he'll have to do. We've got to be practical, especially now. But not the woman."

Josh and Gale had been hovering outside the tent.

"Josh, can you take some shots for us?"

"You bet." He smiled and headed for the tent. Gale followed.

"Sorry Gale. Just Josh."

"What's his problem?" Gale fumed.

Rip, busy making notes and measuring, looked up when Josh entered. "Good, you found him. All right, what's your name?"

"Josh Stadler." His toothy grin, shaggy bangs, and laid-back manner almost put Rip at ease. In work boots, faded jeans, and an old green tee-shirt he looked more like a landscaper. Only the Nikon DSLR around his neck and a worn camera bag at his side said otherwise.

"Okay, Josh, do you know how to work that thing?" Rip asked.

"I might be able to figure it out," Josh chuckled. At twenty-nine, Josh had already shot in more countries than Rip had dug in. *National Geographic* recently released his photo book of ancient sites.

"Good. Shoot this from every angle. Get some close-ups of the casing too." Rip placed a hand on Josh's shoulder and looked into his eyes. "But *nothing* is published without my okay. Do we have a deal?"

Josh looked at Larsen, who nodded.

"You got it, Doc," Josh answered, giving a half laugh. Then he went to work, clicking away, but the lighting was bad and the flash just glared off the shiny surface. "Without my lighting equipment these shots won't be any good. We need to take it outside."

"Okay," Rip agreed. They grabbed the card table and placed a roll of duct tape on its side as a stand for the inner sphere. Gale and Rip collided.

"Can we get her out of here?" Rip barked at Larsen.

Gale took in the scene. "Did *that* come *out of* that?" Gale asked, pointing.

Rip ignored her.

"The sun is a little intense. Maybe if I stand on a chair I can avoid some of the shadows," Josh said. Larsen grabbed a small crate that he hoped would support his weight.

Suddenly, lights glowed from within the inner sphere. Everyone jumped back.

4

"It's glowing! What *is* this thing?" Larsen eyed the inner sphere as if it might attack him at any moment.

Rip didn't want to touch it, but several students were heading toward them so he snatched it up and pushed back into the tent. The lights vanished.

"I don't believe what I just saw," Larsen said.

"Did you get it?" Rip asked Josh.

"First rule of photography. When something happens, keep shooting." Josh smiled and showed Rip several shots in the camera's preview window. "I really like this one, how the blue and green lights seem to—"

"I don't care what you like," Rip said. "Larsen, send those students back to the cliff. There might be more still buried."

"Those lights kind of blow your theory, huh Doc?" Josh said.

Rip looked at him incredulously. The Cosega Theory now appeared to be a fact. He might have been too conservative, his radical theory not extreme enough. Nonetheless, the understanding on which all of history and society itself were based now lay shattered among the dirt and pine needles on the forest floor. Intelligent humans had been here much longer than previously thought – unimaginably longer.

"We have to get this out of here. It needs to be studied under lab conditions, without the media and all these students," Rip said as Larsen returned.

"Hey, I hate to burst your bubble, but we're on federal land. We can't just take these artifacts. The government is going to grab these up," Larsen said.

"They don't have to know yet." Rip motioned to the inner-sphere and stone casings of the split globe. "These are far out of the scope of this dig. We just don't tell them."

"We can't."

"Why?"

"You can't risk losing the context of what may possibly be the most important find in history."

"It's exactly because this *is* the most important find in history that I can."

"They need to be dated. They are primary context finds. Within the archaeological matrix, it's impossible. If the limestone formed around the globe casings, the carvings would be filled. It's more like the cliff was used as a vault. I just can't explain the absence of any seams."

"None of that matters right now," Rip argued. "I'm one of the top three archaeologists in the world. I've got a freakin' *National Geographic* team recording every detail, and there are nineteen trained witnesses out there. Showing the context within the archaeological matrix isn't going to be an issue. Rewriting the history books is all anyone is going to need to worry about."

"What about Gale and Josh and all the others who have seen it? How do you propose to keep them quiet?"

"He won't," Gale snapped, barging into the tent.

"Damn it," Rip growled. "The government will screw this up. They'll destroy something that they have no idea about. This is beyond governments—"

Larsen cut him off. "What are you going to do if word does leak out? 'Cause it will."

"I'll drive off that bridge when I get to it."

"You may not care about risking your career, but I do."

"Are you kidding? Look at this thing. This is going to *make* your career. It's going to make you famous, whether we like it or not."

"I'm going to publish this story, Professor Gaines," Gale said. "And it'll read better if you steal artifacts from the government and try to suppress a historic find. So I say do it."

"Why the hell are you here?" Rip shook his head. "They never should have been here, Larsen. That was a cataclysmic mistake."

"I didn't know what we were going to find. Josh, Gale, we just need time," Larsen pleaded.

"Time? Why not just announce the find? You're tops in your field. You can study it all you want," Gale said, half-mimicking him.

"There's more to it." Rip stopped himself. "I can't believe I'm explaining myself to a reporter and a photographer."

"Unprecedented events call for unprecedented actions," Gale said. "How old is this thing, really? What were those lights?"

"That's what I'm saying. I need time to find out," Rip said, frustrated.

"And you didn't answer. Why not go the proper route?" she persisted.

"This is too important to trust with politicians and bureaucrats. Look, I'm not some teenager who found a lost wallet. I could spend the rest of my life working on this single discovery. This will have more impact on the world than Sumer, Gutenberg, the Renaissance, all the wars and religions combined."

"Come on," Josh said, laughing.

"I assure you, I am not prone to exaggeration."

"You give me a complete exclusive, and I'll hold the story for a week," Gale offered.

The urgency in Rip's voice and his willingness to risk his career won her agreement.

"Thirty days," Rip countered.

"Two weeks," Gale said.

Josh didn't have an issue with covering it up. He'd been arrested protesting the wars in Afghanistan and Iraq and would do anything to deny the Republicans something.

"I know you don't want to hear this, but I still think it's wiser to do this through formal channels," Larsen said.

"All I'm asking for is a little time. The federal government is big and clumsy—" Rip began.

"And corruption is rampant," Gale added.

"You know how many routine digs they've screwed up?" Rip continued. "How many artifacts they've 'lost'. Do you want a list?"

"It's a federal offense," Larsen said quietly.

"We're not going to keep it."

"You don't even know what *it* is," Larsen said.

"I know what it isn't," Rip said. "It isn't something that belongs in that cliff. It isn't something from that time! And it sure as hell isn't anything the government knows how to handle."

Larsen stared at him.

"Larsen, it *lit up*," Rip whispered. "You know what they do with stuff like this. It will vanish into the netherworld of the intelligence community's research realm. They'll deny we found anything."

"Do you think this is like Roswell?" Josh asked. "Because this thing could be something like that."

"Do you know what really happened there?" Rip snapped impatiently.

"I know that there are hundreds of trillions of stars out there. And to think that only a single little planet orbiting one of those stars can support intelligent life is a silly notion," Josh said.

"That doesn't mean the US government has been covering up proof of visitors from another planet for nearly seventy years," Rip said.

"It doesn't mean they aren't," Gale said.

"You think this is from another planet?" Larsen asked skeptically.

"No," Rip answered. "But that would make it much easier to explain. It's exactly because I think it's from *this* planet that it's so extraordinary. And for that reason it can't be allowed to fall into the hands of the government until we understand it and figure out its origins."

"It does appear to predate the formation of America by millions of years, so maybe the jurisdiction and ownership issues are a bit fuzzy," Larsen said half-heartedly.

"It predates the origin of *homo sapiens* by millions of years," Rip said. "So you're in? We all agree the government doesn't have to know what we found here?"

"I'm in," Gale said.

Josh nodded. "Yep."

They all looked to Larsen.

"I guess so," he said.

5

The nineteen people involved with the excavation were standing around speculating about the stone globe while the four assigned to that area continued the dig. Larsen tried to downplay the find and explained to the students that the artifacts were being sent out for dating. They hoped this would buy them time without raising suspicion. Fortunately, none of the students had seen the inner sphere or glowing lights.

Meanwhile, Rip planned to take the artifacts to a lab in Maryland where people he trusted could help unravel the mystery. Josh took more photos of the cliff. It was solid limestone except for where the Odeon and the globe had been. More than a hundred test holes had been drilled that yielded nothing else unusual.

"Could the cliff have simply formed around the artifacts?" Josh asked.

"Maybe your little green men from Roswell put them there," Rip answered sarcastically.

Josh laughed. "Good one, Doc."

"It's a fair question, Professor," Gale said.

"It's nothing but questions," Rip shot back. "We have to have the casings tested to verify actual age. I'm not interested in theorizing until we know how old it is."

"I thought you were all about theories, or should I say the Cosega Theory." Gale stared at Rip as a cat does a cornered mouse.

"This is beyond that," he said, glaring back.

"Sure, but doesn't it prove your crazy theory?"

"Nothing is proven until it is proven."

Gale laughed. "Profound, Professor."

The heat of the day still lingered as darkness encroached on the camp. Earlier, Larsen had a tent cleared for Rip. Ever since, he'd been reviewing the images and making notes on his laptop. The smoke of burning hickory and pine flavored the air as the dinner fires began to diminish.

"Can you spare a moment, Professor?"

He recognized Gale's voice. He didn't really dislike *her*, he disliked her presence and the complications she and Josh added to the equation. Now that she had agreed to keep a lid on the story, he was trying to be friendlier.

"Come in." He minimized the screens so his computer revealed only a wallpaper of Machu Picchu.

She sat in a canvas chair across from him. "I haven't changed my mind about holding the story, but I can't believe you don't know what we discovered today."

He wanted to respond sarcastically, noting she wasn't part of the "we" who discovered anything. Instead, her eyes softened him.

"I don't actually know," he admitted.

"Off the record." She moved her chair closer and whispered, "You've been looking for something to prove Cosega . . . this is it, right?"

Rip wanted her to leave, but needed her cooperation. "I am not looking for the Holy Grail or another tomb of Tutankhamen. It's true that I have theories that need to be transformed into facts, and the only way to do that is to unearth evidence, but it's more a quest than a single strike."

"Come on, Professor. I saw your face when that ball lit up."

"Anytime the past lifts the veil and gives us something it's an exciting moment."

She smiled. "This is more than that Professor. Just tell me."

He looked past her, searching his thoughts for an answer. "I can't."

"My years covering Wall Street taught me how to tell when someone is concealing something. You know more than you're saying."

"I wouldn't be telling you anything if you weren't here."

"But I am here."

"Look, why don't you just leave this story alone? I already promised you an exclusive."

"You want my silence. You're asking me to trust you."

He looked away. Neither spoke for a minute.

"Let me tell you a story," he said. "About twenty years ago there was a discovery of ancient pottery in South America that was an *exact* match to Egyptian pottery of the same period." He scowled. "A prominent magazine published the finding, and within days of the issue hitting the stands the site was completely looted and several archaeologists were murdered." His voice rose. "It was a vital clue in our search for the past that made Tutankhamen seem trivial, yet it's gone and good men died. We'll never know how much we lost from the artifacts and the men." He stood. "Don't you see? Without understanding the truth of human history, we are adopted, wandering, and lost. Trust me, Gale."

"Okay," she said, "but trust is a two-way street. There is a reason I'm here. Let me find out why."

Falling asleep later that night, Rip thought about the inner sphere and decided to call it "Eysen," an ancient word meaning, "to hold all the stars in your hand." At the same time a far less important, yet still nagging question distracted him.

Why the hell is Gale Asher here?

6

The Special Agent studied his notes again. It didn't make sense. He'd actually heard of Ripley Gaines. He'd read an article in *Newsweek* or somewhere once, some sort of modern-day, real-life Indiana Jones. But, as required, he called a superior at the Bureau and through a series of decisions up the chain of command, it landed on the Director's desk within an hour. The circumstances were strange enough to stand out. That's what always got the FBI's attention – things out of the norm. And a renowned archaeologist concealing a major find on federal lands seemed very odd.

Larsen put down the sandwich he'd been eating and found his ringing satphone. He listened carefully, became increasingly alarmed, and ran to Rip's tent.

"We're in trouble," he said, bursting in on Rip who had just returned from a final look at the cliff and was preparing to leave. "One of the grad students left the camp an hour ago. He's got a girlfriend at the University of Virginia. As soon as he hit the main road he stopped to fill up with gas. The feds were there."

"What feds?" Rip asked, confused.

"An SUV packed with FBI agents pulled up and met a Forest Service vehicle. He heard a man in a suit talking to the ranger about an archaeological site. He didn't get all of the discussion, but he said they're definitely headed for the camp."

"That's crazy. How would they know?"

"I know that gas station. They'll be here in less than forty-five minutes."

"How the hell do they know!?" Rip repeated.

"One of the students must have told someone," Larsen said.

"But how? Who? There's no cell coverage here. You and I are the only ones with satphones. Did anyone else leave?"

"No way. But what does it matter? We haven't done anything wrong. We'll just report the find. It's not a big deal."

He looked at Larsen with disdain. "Are you kidding? Nothing has changed."

Rip wrapped the Odeon and the Eysen in flannel shirts from his luggage, then carefully placed them into his backpack along with the top of the casing.

"What are you doing?"

"I'm sure as hell not sticking around here."

"There's no way out. One road in and they're on it. Come on Rip, don't be crazy. It'll all work out. We're about to be famous. Well, you're already famous, but this is going to be Oprah-famous. *People Magazine*, 60 Minutes, they may even make us *Time Magazine* people of the year."

"Larsen, don't you see? The fact that they're sending agents up here less than twenty-four hours after we pulled the globe out of the ground shows that this is too important to hand over."

"Come on, Rip. You're being paranoid."

"Damn it, Larsen, how long have you known me? We don't have time to debate this anymore. You're just going to have to trust me."

Larsen nodded silently. "I can't stop you, but I can't be a part of this either."

"Okay."

Ten minutes had already been lost. The black SUV and the Forest Service vehicle were down there somewhere, winding their way along the old logging road that Rip had come up the day before.

Rip found Josh and Gale and gave them the news.

"Can I hide the bottom section of the stone casing somewhere in your car?" he asked Josh.

"Sure. But what if they search it?"

"Why would they search it?" Rip asked. "Besides, I don't know what else to do."

After a couple of minutes looking for the best spot, they decided on the spare tire compartment. Rip jogged to his tent for his notes where Gale caught up to him.

"I'm going with you," she said.

"I don't think so!"

"Then stop me."

This was a complication he didn't need. Who in the hell did she think she was? He pushed past her, heading breathlessly into the forest. They both knew time did not allow for an argument, so he planned to lose her in the climb. By the time the SUV pulled into camp, Gale and Rip were halfway up the first ridge.

Six suits wearing shades climbed out of the government vehicle. They asked for Ripley Gaines. Students directed them from one tent to another until it became clear he had slipped away.

"Damn," Wayne Hall, the senior agent and the only African-American in the group, said as he pushed a button on his satphone. Within thirty minutes, a helicopter arrived and four more vehicles were on their way to the Thomas Jefferson National Forest.

Dixon Barbeau emerged from the helicopter, already disliking the case. Years earlier, hunting a fugitive in the mountains had cost him his marriage. He couldn't help but recall the frustrating, five-year manhunt for Eric Rudolph that had bogged down his early career.

Hall's mood matched his superior's. They'd worked together before, and Hall dreaded the days ahead if they didn't catch Ripley Gaines quickly. Less than five percent of the FBI's special agents were African-American, and Hall got the sense that Barbeau resented that the number was that high. He also considered Barbeau outrageously arrogant.

Recently his girlfriend had been teaching him deep breathing relaxation techniques. He took in a long breath, held it, exhaled, then joined Barbeau.

Eight more agents ran, stooping, from the copter. While Hall briefed him, Barbeau shouted orders. The agents cordoned off the camp, rounded up everyone, began questioning, and collected "evidence." Larsen nervously stared at Barbeau – six-three, short blond hair, perfect smile, and piercing eyes. He looked more like a combination of an angry marine and a Senate candidate than an FBI Special Agent. The feds had already taken over the largest tent and turned it into a mini-command center. It felt suffocating to Larsen.

"Professor . . ." Barbeau checked an iPad, "Fretwell. Larsen Fretwell. Would you like to explain just what is going on here?"

"This is an accredited archaeological dig. We have a USFS special use permit. Perhaps I should be asking *you* what's going on. Why is the FBI hassling us?"

Barbeau's eyes narrowed as he swallowed a laugh. "Really? You think we're hassling you? How about you tell me where Dr. Ripley Gaines and the artifacts he stole from federal land are? Why don't you tell me what those artifacts *are?*"

"I think I need a lawyer."

"I think you need a really good one. We're not the Mayberry PD here. The 'F' in FBI means you've stepped in it deep. You're an accomplice in a federal crime, and do you know what irritates me more than the humid summers in Virginia? *Liars*. So, no disrespect Professor, but why don't you start over. And this time turn on that highly trained brain of yours."

"I would like to speak with an attorney."

"I'll see if I can find one for you," Barbeau said, sarcastically. "Wait here."

He left Larsen sitting there, dry-mouthed and shaken.

As the students went through the process of being photographed, identified, and questioned, Josh Stadler showed his press credentials and was "allowed" to leave after he turned over his camera's memory cards. His car got a quick once-over, but nothing was found.

Hall reported better results from the student interrogations. They ascertained that Ripley Gaines and Gale Asher had been in the camp at least half an hour before Hall's group arrived, and since the pair hadn't been passed on the road, the fugitives had clearly left on foot. In less than an hour the sun would set, so there wasn't much point in sending a pursuit team into the forest. The big search would have to wait until first light, but Hall did get a couple sharpshooters up in the air. They might get lucky.

7

A wet spring had left the July foliage thick, making the temperature at least fifteen degrees cooler in the forest. Gale and Rip hardly slowed. The quiet collapsed as the first helicopter circled. Rip kept running while he searched the heavy canopy.

Gale's eyes met his. "How did they know?"

Rip shook his head and continued moving, his single mission to protect the artifacts. After a lifetime of searching, the inconceivable secrets he'd been promised were about to be revealed.

Barbeau always had a plan. "Freedom," he said to Hall. "The tactic never fails. Allow a suspect to think he's free, like he got away with something, and he'll end up giving up everything – unintentionally, of course."

Hall nodded. He knew how to play it.

"Professor Larsen Fretwell, I'm Special Agent Hall."

"You must be the good cop. Well, let me save you the trouble. I've already told Mr. bad cop Barbeau that I have nothing to say until I get an attorney."

"Sure thing. You're free to go," Hall said.

Larsen couldn't hide his surprise.

"Turns out I really am the good cop." Hall smiled. "But let me caution you that you are a person of interest in a federal investigation and are not to leave the country. We don't have enough evidence to arrest or detain you yet. However, you will likely be asked to come in for questioning. You can, of course, bring your lawyer at that time."

Twenty-five minutes later, Larsen drove out of camp, desperately scanning the woods for Rip. Three vehicles filled with the students followed him. With the entire crew gone, the camp now belonged to the FBI.

Gale and Rip maintained their exhausting pace. Just as darkness descended, they emerged onto a narrow dirt road that looked as if it hadn't seen a vehicle in a decade and might be better described as a wide trail.

"Where does it go?" Gale asked as Rip turned the forest service map in several directions.

"It's not on the map, but it seems to be going north, which works for us." He shoved the map back in his pocket. "More importantly, we can follow it at night."

They hadn't talked much as they tried to put distance between themselves and the camp. The Eysen and the many possible explanations for its origins almost completely occupied Rip's mind. That, and being overwhelmed by his life-destroying decision to run. He knew next to nothing about the artifacts in his pack, but he knew enough to risk everything to save them.

Having Gale along added several complications though, and she might not be easy to lose. A yoga enthusiast, Gale normally hiked several miles a day, ate only macrobiotic foods, and thus had no trouble keeping up with the strapping archaeologist.

Although they continued their hurried pace along the dirt road, not having to bushwhack through the underbrush made their flight easier. The night, dimly lit by a half-moon breaking through the canopy, was warm and sticky.

"How do you think they found out about the discovery?" Gale asked again. The question had nagged at Rip since Larsen told him government agents were converging on the camp. He assumed someone had accidentally told the wrong person.

"You're the reporter. What do you think?"

"I have no idea, but weren't there only two satphones in camp?"

"Yeah, mine and Larsen's."

"Was yours ever out of your control?"

"No."

"Then whoever notified the government must have used Larsen's satphone."

"It's not Larsen, if that's what you're thinking," he said, his eyes darting. At that moment, mountain lions and bears worried him more than figuring out who had tipped the federal agents.

"I'm just saying his satphone was the only way to get word out of the camp. That narrows the choices. And Larsen was very reluctant to go along with taking the artifacts."

"It's *not* him."

"Well it sure would be nice to know *who* turned us in." Gale sipped her water. "You realize that they turned us in before we even did anything. I'm afraid only the two of us, Josh, and Larsen knew we were going to conceal it."

"It wasn't Larsen. He believes in Cosega almost as much as I do. Will you just drop it?"

"I guess someone might have heard us talking?"

"Damn it, it could have been anyone. Right now, I'm more worried about the morning. They'll certainly bring in search teams and do more flyovers. We need to get out of the mountains."

"Cosega is an old Indian word meaning 'before the beginning,' right?"

"Yes," Rip said, glad she'd changed the subject, but still

wished she'd shut up. "Most Native American cultures' creation stories begin long before the European versions."

"Meaning they were here more than twenty thousand years ago?"

"Right."

"So you think some ancestors of Monacan or Cherokee put those artifacts in the cliff."

"No, I don't think that. Do you ever stop talking?"

"Did it really light up? How could something buried for millions of years light up?"

"That's why we're running."

They didn't talk again for a while. The weight of their situation was enough to carry. Walking, thinking, the coolness of the night, and with the apprehension of the approaching dawn, each step grew heavier.

If Barbeau had known more about what they found, there would have been soldiers with night goggles in the forest, hundreds of them. But he didn't have enough information. Still, the Director of the FBI had called twice. For some reason, the higher-ups were watching this one. By nightfall, he had transformed the camp into a full-fledged command center with even more experts on the way.

In the coming days the government archaeologists would sift, drill, chisel, and dig the cliff down to almost nothing. Rip's reputation in the scientific community told them the find had to be incredibly significant. One prominent scientist described Rip's apparent willingness to throw away a brilliant career for an artifact, as "mindboggling."

8

Josh was worried about Gale. He didn't understand the government's swift and forceful presence at the dig site. He debated whether he should still deliver the casing, but in the end decided it would be the most responsible thing to do. They weren't stealing an antiquity to sell on the black market. They were trying to preserve the items for further scientific study. He habitually checked the rearview mirror, paranoid about the FBI following him.

During the three-hour drive to Bethesda, Maryland, he made three important phone calls. First, he arranged to meet Rip's contact at the lab at seven the following morning. Second, he called someone he never would have dreamt of talking to before Rip handed him a card with only "Booker H. Lipton" and a phone number printed in black. Josh's instructions were to tell Booker that Rip had made a find of vital importance and to explain that there was trouble with the feds. Rip might be in touch with Lipton at any time and would need his help in disappearing.

Third, he spoke with his brother Sean, who found the whole drama very exciting. Sean Stadler's zest for life had led him into adventures and mishaps since they were kids. Sean needed no convincing to break away from his summer classes at nearby Lynchburg College to do Josh a favor. The two lanky brothers were very close, and even with a seven-year age difference could pass as twins. They were both constantly tan, always smiling big toothy grins, goofy flirts with women, and raised to be counted on. Especially by family and friends.

Rip felt as if he was running from Gale's questions as they stumbled through the darkness. Her curiosity about the Cosega Theory continued.

"You already know what my theory is," he said.

"Sure, but like everyone else, I thought you were a little— "

"Crazy?"

"It wasn't even that I thought you were nuts. I just always thought you were trying to get attention."

"You reporters never understood me. Attention was the *last* thing I wanted."

"Then why did you publish?"

"Because it's true."

"And?"

"I expected to draw out other scientists pursuing the same conclusions, someone with proof. Instead, all I found were crackpots and suddenly my peers began to shun me. And the media, you people were the worst. You acted as if I'd just claimed to have flown on a UFO."

"Don't lump me in with the haters."

"Why not? You've been harassing me since we first met."

"Poor baby." Gale chuckled. "You have to admit that without proof, and not another single scientist in the world backing your thesis, it's a little wild."

"Someone always has to go first. Change scares people."

"Reminds me of what Gandhi said, '*First they ignore you. Then they laugh at you. Then they fight you. Then you win.'* I believe you, Rip."

"Sure. You do now because you saw an eleven-million-year-old artifact light up."

"Yes, but how can you prove its age?"

"They have new techniques. LAD stands for Laser Astronomical Dating. It works with known geological data. It's complicated, but effective in cases like this."

"Are there other cases like *this?* What you found seems like a classic OOPArt."

"Out-of-place artifact," Rip said, raising his eyebrows and with a slight frown. "You do surprise with your obscure knowledge. But most OOPArts, that is artifacts found in an impossible context, are hoaxes. I assure you these items are real."

"You believe so deeply in your theory that you've given up everything for it."

"I didn't really give up anything. Cosega is my life. I never really had a choice."

"We always have a choice. Why do you say Cosega is your life?"

A cool breeze took him back to the mountains of his youth, filled with mysteries and adventure. Rip recalled the discovery he'd made as a teenager, so powerful that it had charted the course of his life, forced him to seek Cosega. But telling a reporter about that was something Rip could not imagine doing.

"I'm certain of two things. The planet is more than 4.5 billion years old, and in spite of what conventional science believes, ours is not the first civilization to flourish."

"How can you be so certain when no one else is?"

"There are more who believe. Larsen for one, and I could name a dozen others."

"Are they all current or past students of yours?"

"Yes, but—"

"Maybe I should call them 'disciples'."

Rip, finished with talking, stomped on ahead. It was true

that most of his allies were culled from the brightest students for whom questioning authority came naturally. Not even Larsen knew how Rip knew for sure, but they believed him because he, likely the brightest archaeologist alive, was unwavering. He pointed to hundreds of finds that had been suppressed to fit current beliefs, but it was his "knowing" that was compelling and irresistible to those who worked closely with him.

For eight years he and Larsen had revised the Cosega Theory, compared notes, and even taken several working vacations together, until Rip published. He became even more famous. His work had been important, and the radical theory couldn't be ignored even though it was ridiculed. Without proof, he risked becoming an outcast in his field, a hero only to quacks and conspiracy theorists. Even his greatest supporter, Booker Lipton, had urged him not to publish without proof.

"Did you hear that?" Gale asked suddenly.

"What?"

"Footsteps."

Rip scanned the night. He and Gale stood fixed, as if they were trees themselves, trying to hear. Every twig, cricket, tree frog, and all those unidentifiable forest sounds were amplified by the blackness, exhaustion, and fear.

"I don't hear anything. I mean other than the African jungle. It could have been a bear."

"Thanks. I was just worried it might be the FBI, but now I have bears to think about."

"Either way, let's pick up the pace."

They continued into the small hours of the morning, lost in their weary thoughts. Rip reviewed all that he knew of human origins and tried to craft a narrative to explain the existence of the Eysen, which blew even his Cosega Theory apart. He wanted to talk to Larsen. No one understood it as much as he did. It was a shame they'd disagreed so intently on the way to handle the artifacts. Still, it was fitting that Larsen had actually found the proof. It made him almost an equal stakeholder in Cosega. They had both worked so hard, but neither had been prepared for the shocking age of their find.

Gale explored her own reasons for following Rip into the mountains. The "story" alone wasn't worth all this, but something from her past also made chasing the Eysen and Cosega nearly as unavoidable for her as it was for Rip.

Wednesday July 12th

Rip fidgeted with his boots. Dew had soaked through to his socks. The sun had risen over a dark peak across the deep valley, making the sky more pink than blue. Their road/trail had been hugging a ridge for the past hour, now with first light it afforded them a three-hundred-sixty-degree view. Gale marveled at the poetry before them, but knew the sun was an enemy.

"Look," Rip said, pulling her to the ground. Not too far away they could see a helicopter taking off. "That's coming from the camp."

"You mean we've only come that far?" Gale asked, defeated.

"We've got to get back into the forest. Come on!"

They sprinted into the safety of the trees. As the shadows receded, Rip found what he was looking for on the map, about two miles away. They jogged around tall pines, heavy oaks, and majestic beech trees until thirty minutes later, giant boulders occupied the forest like an army. The huge stones, some forty or fifty feet high, came from nowhere, competing with the trees for space.

"It's like another world," Gale said as the boulders completely took over the landscape, forming caves, tunnels, pits, and bridges.

"This is Indian Rocks. A sacred site for a long-forgotten tribe."

Gale reached for Rip's shoulder. "It's remarkable."

"Professor Gaines," a loud male voice said from somewhere in the stone maze.

Rip dropped silently to the ground. Gale froze.

They tried to find the source of the voice. There was a blur of movement, crunching leaves, and footsteps. "Hey, Professor Gaines?"

Rip didn't know the voice and still couldn't see anybody.

"Professor? Gale? It's Sean Stadler. Josh's brother!" he shouted.

Gale exhaled in relief.

"We're trying to *avoid* attention," Rip called out softly.

"Oh, yeah, right. Sorry. I wasn't sure you were here yet."

They met next to two round stones the size of mini-vans. "You look just like Josh," Gale said, hugging him.

"I'm actually the better looking one, but he's a little smarter so it equals out," Sean joked, showing off his dimples.

"Let's get to your car," Rip said. "There's no time."

"Sure. I'm parked about two or three minutes away. Slid my Jeep right behind a Park Service maintenance shed. Can't even see it from the road," Sean said, smiling at Gale and hoping she'd be impressed with his cleverness.

A loud thwopping roar suddenly sent terror through them – the unmistakable sound of a military helicopter flying in fast and low. The upper branches of the tall trees whipped around as it hovered.

9

Rip, Gale, and Sean rushed into a stone tunnel. The chopper circled above them.

"Damn it, it must have seen us," Rip said above the steady drumbeat of the rotors.

"How could they through all the trees?" Gale asked.

"Who knows what kind of imaging equipment they've got?"

Rip considered their options. Escaping on foot might be best. In the vast forest they might be able to get away before agents caught up, but they had to try for the car. If they needed to, they could always abandon the vehicle later and slip back into the trees.

"Listen," Gale said, stopping suddenly. "It's going away."

The chopper moved off to the west and repeated its pattern. Still, the incessant sound of rotating blades and churn of the Blackhawk's engine would continue to haunt them.

The irreparable damage Rip had done to his career was one thing. The possibility that he could wind up in prison hit him like a wave of food poisoning. In all his years of searching for a Cosega find he'd assumed there would be some resistance at the new view of our past, but he never expected to be hunted like an animal.

"Rip, are you okay?" Gale asked.

"No," he said. Exhaustion and tension gnawed at him. His legs burned. She thought his eyes were teary, but he started jogging. "We've got to get to the car!" he shouted.

They darted across the sleepy Blue Ridge Parkway.

Sean's ten-year-old, primer-grey Jeep looked like an oasis, but the relief was fleeting. They knew agents were fanning out through the forest. Roadblocks were being coordinated, and more helicopters . . . this would be a long day.

"Where to?"

Gale answered, "Asheville, North Carolina." She looked back at Rip.

He nodded. Their plan, hatched in the night, seemed less likely to succeed now with the reality of a closing net around them.

"What's in Asheville?" Sean asked, but didn't wait for an answer. "I knew a girl there once. Pretty place."

Rip held his pack across his lap. "Look, Sean, I don't want to be rude, but it's really not a good idea to tell you too much."

"Sure, sure." Sean smiled in the rearview mirror, giving Rip a wink. "I'm cool. The cloak and dagger stuff is no problem. We'll play it however you want, Professor."

The forty-five-mile-per-hour speed limit in the nation's busiest national park made Rip nervous. The park was actually a four hundred and sixty-nine mile road. They needed to go faster, but he told Sean to keep it at forty-eight.

Four more government SUVs arrived at the camp, now overrun with close to forty government employees from various agencies. Barbeau and Hall reviewed the reports coming in from various field agents.

"Larsen Fretwell got a room at the Ty River Motel in Nelson County, Virginia. He tried calling Ripley Gaines' satphone six times. Gaines has it shut off and must have the battery out because we've been unable to trace it." Hall scrolled his tablet. "This morning Fretwell started driving north approximately thirty minutes ago, just stopped at a diner."

Barbeau just grunted. The tent was stuffy as the morning rose, and he had a bad feeling this might not wrap up quickly.

"Fretwell doesn't seem to be in a hurry. He's not running. His background is completely clean. Maybe we should pick him up and do a thorough questioning. He might say more with an attorney holding his hand."

Barbeau glared at Hall. "This guy is much more use to us out there making noise."

"Do we have a motive theory yet?"

Barbeau had thought about it all night, and knew the question would be asked repeatedly during the day by his superiors, but it annoyed him that Hall had asked. "They found a priceless artifact. Gaines is greedy."

Hall nodded. They both knew it wouldn't satisfy anyone, but Hall didn't really want to wade into that mess yet with Barbeau. Still, it bothered him. He'd heard of Gaines even before reading his file. Gaines showed up on TV any time an archaeological story made the news. He had no known drug, alcohol, or gambling issues. He didn't even have a wife. A major publisher had signed him to a two-book deal. The first, "*The Future of the Past*," would be released in three months. Hall had just subpoenaed a copy of the manuscript. This kind of man doesn't steal artifacts. He could make more money talking and writing about them.

"Just because his motives aren't obvious, doesn't mean the guy isn't crooked. By the end of the day we'll know a lot more," Barbeau said, leaving the tent. He walked to the cliff and spoke with a government archaeologist who had been working with an agent on compiling scientific data and a schedule of facts to be included in a report for higher-ups.

Hall caught up and as they stood looking around at the bustling camp. He struggled to voice his concern.

"You have something else?" Barbeau asked, sensing Hall's apprehension.

"It's just . . . the bureau has escalated this case to an extreme level. Literally overnight."

"So?"

"This guy's not a terrorist. There's no justification for these kinds of resources being utilized on what's really nothing more than a theft."

"I'll let the Director know you disagree with how he's running the agency when I speak to him later."

"Barbeau, why don't you get the chip off your shoulder so you can see a little more clearly? How many cases have you been on where the Director oversees like this?"

"I haven't had this kind of interference since the Rudolph case," Barbeau admitted.

"Exactly. And that was a media circus. The Director had to watch every step. That guy had killed people and was a known bomber. We're looking for a scientist who took some old carved ball out of the dirt. The media doesn't even know it happened."

"They probably expect the media to get wind of it soon. I'm sure the Director will brief me later. I'll keep you in the loop."

Barbeau had been hiding his anxiety from the start. He'd been with the bureau for twenty-eight years, but something was wrong with this case. Even the way the FBI first got involved didn't add up. He hoped the Director would have answers.

Josh rubbed his aching head and shifted uncomfortably in a green vinyl and chrome chair. It had been a fitful night in a chain motel room with bad TV. The cramped waiting room smelled of pine cleaner. He wanted to meet Ian Sweedler, give him the casing, and be done with this business. Josh worried that involving Sean had been a bad idea, and was thinking of calling him when Ian Sweedler, looking as if he'd been born and raised in a lab, walked in. His white coat, oversized glasses, and shiny, prematurely-balding head screamed nerdy science geek, but there was a warmth about him.

"How long have you been working for Professor Gaines?" Ian asked while they walked back to an employees' break room.

"I'm actually a photographer. Just doing a favor for a friend, "Josh said. He carefully unwrapped the casing from an old blanket.

Sweedler stepped back. "Ginodino! Is there another half to this thing?" He whistled. "Was there anything inside?"

"I have no idea," Josh lied.

"Rip is always finding the coolest stuff. Do we know anything about where, how, when it was found?"

"I don't know a thing, I'm just the messenger. But Rip said it is extremely important and he needs an age as soon as possible."

"Don't worry. I owe Rip a few favors. I'll get it fast-tracked."

Josh hesitated, reluctant to leave it, but Rip had said Ian could be trusted. He gave Sweedler his cell phone number.

Back on the Washington Beltway, Josh tried calling his brother, but Sean was out of range. He checked his voice mail. "Why haven't they called?" he asked out loud.

He didn't notice the car following him.

10

The United States Attorney General, Harrison Dover, leafed through the report. He found the description of the stone globe disturbing. None of it made sense to him. He knelt and prayed, as he did every morning with his staff. Dover, a devout Catholic, often shared information with contacts at the Vatican. He knew that next to Israel, the most reliable intelligence network in the world belonged to the Vatican. These days the US needed all the help they could get.

Dover wanted to know what the church scholars thought of this strange event – a renowned archaeologist uncovering and then absconding with an artifact that appeared to predate even Darwin's theories of the history of man. A source reported that Gaines had declared the discovery would rewrite church history, but Dover had heard claims like that his whole life. So it surprised him when a Cardinal in Rome phoned to request an urgent meeting.

Three hours later, Dover ushered Francesco Pisano, a Vatican representative, into his office. They discussed the status of the case, and Pisano conveyed the Pope's interest in the artifacts. Pisano liked people to know he knew the Pope, but he'd really only met him once. He actually answered to a man more than a dozen rungs down the Vatican ladder. Pisano was a pious man who took his job seriously, even if he didn't understand the nuances of each order given to him. But he followed them precisely to avoid making mistakes. The Church didn't like things botched, and Pisano had a solid record of cleaning up and avoiding messes. He didn't know it yet, but the Eysen was the most important case he'd ever been assigned, and meeting with the United States Attorney General gave him some idea of the gravity. He suddenly felt very important.

"Forgive me, Francesco," Dover said to the small, balding man, "but I don't understand why an unseen object dug from the forest of the Virginia mountains could possibly concern the Holy Father."

"It's a matter on which I've not been fully briefed. Several Cardinals will arrive from Italy tomorrow to provide more details. However, I assure you if it wasn't of the utmost priority to the Pope, then I would not have been called in to meet with you," Pisano said while evaluating the Attorney General's suit, unsure if it was nicer than his own. He considered style critical to success, and spent more on clothes than his budget should allow. In the end, he decided his Armani was better than Dover's Ralph Lauren.

"You're asking me to escalate an investigation, commit considerable resources—"

"The Holy See is making this request," Pisano corrected. "Haven't I been clear?"

"Yes." Dover squinted at Pisano. "I'm of course inclined to grant this favor. However, I'll need more to go on. I don't operate in a vacuum."

"It should be enough that I am here on behalf of the Pope."

Dover, a powerful man, was not used to being stonewalled, and that's just what he believed Pisano was doing. But the Attorney General was also a practical and skilled politician, and the recent news reports speculating that he could be a future vice presidential candidate were inaccurate only in that they underestimated his ambitions.

A silence hung in the room.

"You are Catholic."

Dover nodded.

"Your Pope has asked."

But it wasn't his deep faith and loyalty to the Church that caused Dover to yield. It was the possibility that a terrifying chain of events may have begun with Gaines' discovery. Pisano had been vague, and alluded to prophecies from secret texts long concealed within the high walls of the world's smallest country surrounded by Rome.

"We've been vigilant in recent years, hoping it would never happen, but carefully watching for any hints. Now it seems we are witnessing its beginning." Pisano's words made Dover shudder.

Pisano had been unwilling to leave until he had received promises from Dover that, among other things, included complete disclosure to the Vatican. Pisano left with digital copies of all the files, and a complete set of the photos they'd recovered from Josh Stadler's camera. "We're not sure the agents got all of his memory cards. There are no close-ups of the artifact, even though we have testimony that some were taken," Dover told him.

Pisano, disappointed, made a note, his mood tempered only by the fact that the Attorney General's Florsheim shoes were no match for his Versaces.

Afterwards, Dover called the Director of the FBI, who in turn immediately sent word to Barbeau's supervisor that the search for Ripley Gaines would no longer be a minor case. Apprehending Gaines and recovering the artifacts were now the Bureau's highest priorities.

"No noise," Dover had told the Director. "I don't want to see this in the *Post*."

The call had been short, as both the Attorney General and

the FBI Director were on their way into meetings. But the Director, surprised by the development, had asked the Attorney General what warranted the unprecedented escalation.

"National Security. More later," had been his terse reply. "How long can this take, Director? You've got a bumbling college professor and some two-bit reporter running through the woods with an old stone ball. Get it done."

Barbeau's stomach tightened. Being in charge of a priority case rarely ended well, and one which needed to stay secret increased the chances for disaster. His only hope to avoid a career damaging hit would be a swift capture. The net widened. They scrutinized, questioned, and watched anyone closely connected to Rip, Gale, Larsen, or the Stadler brothers. An hour after Barbeau got word, the Director himself phoned for an update and ended the call with a firm directive.

"Wrap up Gaines within twenty-four hours. This guy is an amateur."

11

Pisano received regular updates from Dover's office, but his superiors in Rome believed the FBI wasn't always efficient, or at least didn't utilize the full range of options available to the Church. Ever since Gaines had published Cosega, the Church had been developing a sophisticated plan to discredit him. However, an actual find would require more drastic measures.

The Vatican had numerous agents in the States, and normally Pisano would have been free to choose which were best suited for the mission. However, everything about this situation was different, and Rome insisted that Joe Nanski be used. Nanski and his partner, Mark Leary, both in their early forties, had worked together for years, helping the Church with a variety of jobs from security and advance work for papal visits, to investigating and discrediting countless sexual abuse allegations against priests. The pair had proved loyal, discreet, and effective.

Pisano knew both men well, and briefed them while driving to a large, suburban church in Vienna, Virginia. Leary, a fanatic who believed all non-Catholics were working against God, made him a little nervous. He grew up in a Catholic orphanage, always dreaming of playing professional football and eventually earning a full athletic scholarship to Notre Dame, becoming a standout on, and off the field. The New York Jets drafted him, but near the end of a brilliant rookie year, Leary blew out his knee.

With his football dreams destroyed, he contemplated suicide. Only working with youth charities gave his life purpose. The Church had saved him. His faith and involvement deepened, and eventually led him to a post with a high-ranking Cardinal. By the time he turned thirty, he was recruited into the Vatican's Secret Police.

For Nanski, the brain to Leary's brawn, life had taken a different course. He studied to be a priest before meeting his future wife, after which he became a religious scholar. Over the years, as more cases required his knowledge, he'd been granted access to an incredible range of historical texts. Although slim, wearing eye-glasses, and with a generally wimpish appearance, the "Bible nerd," as his wife called him, was no less passionate about his faith, and would do whatever was required to protect the Church, including to kill.

The two men had met six years earlier while on a sticky case that involved untangling a bishop from Mafia extortion, and had become friends. Both possessed the critical ingredient needed by a servant of the Church: absolute devotion.

After breakfast, still unable to reach Rip, Larsen phoned Josh and told him what happened at the camp after he left with the hidden casing.

"Where are Gale and Rip?" he asked.

"I was hoping you knew. I got the casing to the lab this morning. My brother should have picked them up hours ago. What if they got arrested? I never should have gotten my brother into this," Josh said while navigating heavy traffic, trying to get to Interstate 95.

"Sean will be all right. Rip is a brilliant guy. He'll figure out how to get away. Even if they get caught, Sean is just giving a ride to his brother's friends. No crime there."

"I wish I shared your optimism. Sean usually doesn't need any help finding trouble, if you know what I mean."

Larsen let out a stilted laugh.

"What really bothers me though is how the FBI found out so fast. They were on the forest road before Gale and Rip even took the artifacts," Josh said.

"I know. Rip should have done this the proper way. He didn't just screw up *his* career. I'm going to have to deal with this affecting my future as well."

They agreed to meet a few hours later at Josh's house in Fredericksburg, Virginia. No longer camping at the dig site, Larsen needed a place to stay and didn't want to return home to Florida until he knew what had happened to Gale, Rip, and the artifacts. Larsen, still angry at what had happened since his find, had been surprised by his friend's actions. In all the years they'd worked together on the Cosega Theory, he'd always known him to be meticulous. But at the same time he'd been aware of Rip's obsession with finding proof. It always seemed as if Rip was searching for something he himself had lost.

A technician had recorded every word of the conversation between Larsen and Josh and immediately contacted Barbeau. Less than half an hour later, agents interviewed classmates who knew Sean Stadler. They brought his girlfriend in for questioning and scared her. Forty minutes after that, a black SUV pulled up to the Bethesda lab. At first Ian denied all knowledge, but the agents, armed with search warrants, knew too much. Even after they had the casing, Ian watched in horror as they tore apart the lab looking for anything else. They released him after a grueling interrogation with instructions not to leave town.

The "artifact" would be at FBI headquarters within forty-five minutes. Barbeau enjoyed the victory. "It's only a matter of time," he told Hall. Still, he worried that it didn't completely match the description the students had given. Gaines must have the other half.

"We agree," Hall said, "that they were tipped off prior to our raid on the dig site. Then why, if his motive *was* theft, did Gaines risk, or even bother with sending half of the priceless artifact out to a lab? The date could have been determined anytime."

That same thought already troubled Barbeau.

"Even the government's archaeologists say the dig protocols were impeccable, and the witnesses all insist that oval thing Gaines called an Odeon and the globe came out of the cliff. The initial findings put the age of the limestone foundation between ten and eleven million years old."

"It's not possible. Look at this thing." Barbeau pointed to the photo on his iPad. "This object is clearly created by an intelligent and skilled human. There weren't any around ten million years ago."

"It's not even close. One of the experts told me that detailed stone carvings have been done for only a few thousand years. And all those perfect circles are precise, like a laser cut them."

"Gaines is a smart man. He isn't going to simply run off with some precious artifact from a dig and sell it. He'd never get away with that. But what about an elaborate hoax? You've read the file. Gaines has a controversial theory he's been trying to prove."

"The Cosega Theory."

"Right. So it's eroding his reputation in the field. He's got a book coming out. It's make or break time in his career. He orchestrates a bogus find that could confirm his theory," Barbeau said impatiently.

"Sounds far-fetched. How does he get away with that?"

"I don't know. Takes an artifact from a dig in Africa and drops it into the woods of Virginia somewhere. He's at the top of his profession. He would know exactly what to do, and few would be able to question him."

"Why risk it? To sell books?"

"No. I'm telling you, his theory borders on quackery. No one else in the scientific community thinks it's possible. He can't back down or he looks stupid, and he can't continue much longer without proof. Gaines is on the verge of losing his grants, his teaching positions, TV appearances, book deal, everything."

Hall shook his head. "I don't know."

"Tell me this. Stealing an artifact, running through the night, are those the normal actions of a stable, upstanding scientist?"

"No."

"Hell no! Those are the acts of a desperate man."

"What about the reporter?" Hall asked.

"She knows a good story when she sees one."

"Maybe. But as far as we can tell, they didn't know each other prior to yesterday. So why would Gaines take her along if he's made it all up?"

"I don't know yet. Gaines has had more time to think about all this than I have. But I'll figure it out. Or I'll catch him first and then make him explain."

Barbeau caught Hall shaking his head again.

"You have a problem with me, Hall?"

"Nope. Just impressed with your confidence."

"You played football in college, right?"

"Tennis."

"Are you joking?"

Hall shook his head.

"Funny. You look like a football player."

"Because I'm black?"

"Yeah. Uh, no. Because you have that solid build thing going on. Look, don't make everything about race. My point is that in football you don't get the touchdowns if you keep looking behind you. I'm heading to the goal line with this case and then I'm going to slam dunk Gaines."

Hall decided to ignore the mixed metaphor.

After its arrival in D.C., technicians shot more than a hundred digital photos of the casing. Moments later, Attorney General Dover reviewed them on his computer, then, as requested, forwarded them to the Vatican. Twenty minutes later, Church scholars carefully studied the shots. Computers ran models and dissected the patterns within the visible carvings. Recommendations moved through a worried hierarchy. They wanted these artifacts.

They woke the Pope.

Somewhere deep below St. Peter's Square, beyond the millions of volumes in the Vatican Library and past the secret archives, a series of vaults, accessible to only a few, housed a collection of scrolls and documents. These hidden texts were so mysterious that only the faintest of rumors across the centuries had kept the possibility of their existence alive.

The photos from the FBI made it necessary for the vaults to be opened for the first time in decades.

12

Pisano got word about the casing as the three Vatican agents pulled into the parking lot of a sprawling brick church. Although the news delighted him, Nanski's mood turned grave when he saw the photo on Pisano's laptop.

Pisano explained the first break in the case, gave them each backpacks, and outlined their mission. Piggy-back on the FBI manhunt, but by God, get to them first. The backpacks contained a couple of satphones, two GPS devices, night goggles, maps, photos of the targets, and, of course, weapons.

"We want the artifacts. Nothing else matters. We don't need the people."

Leary understood the implied instructions, and although he didn't enjoy it, he would, if necessary, kill again for the Church. He believed himself to be a soldier of God, and had no doubt that the ends always justified the means. *Evil is everywhere*, he thought. *Attacks on my church are attacks on me and will be defended.* The former linebacker sucked on an eight-month-old candy cane he had found in a Sunday School teacher's desk. "This brainy dirt-digger is going to be fun to knock around," Leary said.

Pisano glanced across at Nanski with a can-you-keep-him-under-control look.

"Nothing about this one is going to be fun," Nanski said, fidgeting with his Saint Christopher medal.

Twenty minutes after they arrived, Leary and Nanski climbed into a brand new, white Toyota Forerunner and headed west on Interstate 66 toward the Blue Ridge Mountains. Leary drove.

"How do you get your hair that short?" Nanski asked as Leary took off his Notre Dame cap.

"Patience. One hair at a time."

Nanski shook his head. "Is that a cross shaved on your temple?" he asked.

"Sure is."

"You're crazy."

"Crazy for Jesus!" Leary whooped.

Nanski reviewed the initial FBI report and the two updates in the folder. "Professor Ripley Gaines, age thirty-nine, left the research camp on foot with a female reporter, Gale Asher, age thirty-four, at approximately eleven a.m. on Tuesday, July eleventh." Nanski checked his watch. "It's now four-fourteen p.m., July twelfth. They've got a twenty-nine-hour head start. We won't even get to the area for three more hours."

"The feds will probably pick them up before we hit the Blue Ridge Parkway. Why are you so worried?" Leary asked.

"The US government cannot be allowed to have both pieces."

"What *is* that stone thing anyway?"

"Something that could bring down the Vatican."

Leary knew his friend to be cautious and pragmatic. He'd never heard Nanski sensationalize anything. "How?"

"It's part of the prophecies of Saint Malachy."

"But the prophecies of Saint Malachy are a fraud."

"I wish it were so."

"Okay. Even if they are genuine, I've read about them. They don't say anything about an artifact like this."

"You only know of Malachy's prophecy about the Popes, but

he said much more and it concerns our current mission. Malachy predicted this."

"A twelfth century archbishop wrote about Gaines?"

"One of Malachy's hidden prophecies is titled *Phialam Insignem Lapidem Ponetis*. The Latin translates roughly to *stone bowl bearing carvings*."

"But this isn't a bowl. It's part of a globe."

"Malachy is brief in his description, but it is clear. Two bowls together hold the secret."

"What secret?"

"The secret that will end the Church."

Leary gasped.

Pisano had been told enough about the hidden prophecies to convince the Attorney General to cooperate, but he'd never read them. Only a handful ever had. Nanski was one of the few. The two men fell silent for many miles.

If Barbeau believed he would eventually capture the fugitives, Hall felt even less certain about an early victory. The couple's flight had begun thirty hours earlier. Even though they left on foot, any number of roads – Interstates 81 and 64; Highways 11, 60, and 501; the Blue Ridge Parkway; and more than ten secondary routes – were within their hiking range. The Bureau had agents in all the major towns – Lexington, Buena Vista, Lynchburg, Harrisonburg, Roanoke, Staunton – but it was impossible to know in which direction to look. Depending on whether they'd managed to acquire a vehicle, they could already be in any of six states, or even on a plane.

Dozens of local police departments were involved. The cover story cited domestic terrorism. Due to the sensitive nature of the investigation, a complete media blackout had been ordered by the Department of Homeland Security. Barbeau was counting on a slip.

"Criminals always make mistakes. It isn't detective work that gets them, it's their screw-ups," he told Hall. "We know Gaines has a satphone. Gale Asher and Sean Stadler each have cell phones. One call and we'll have them."

"You're forgetting that Gaines has a genius level IQ. Mistakes aren't as likely with him."

"You're forgetting that many criminals are highly intelligent."

"I'm not so sure Gaines is a criminal."

"How did you get this job Hall? Was it an affirmative action thing?"

"Screw you, Barbeau. You think anyone the Bureau is after is a crook. Did you know that the US Constitution says Gaines is innocent until proven guilty?"

"The courts can decide that question. My job is to get the thieving bastard in handcuffs so that they can sentence him to jail time."

Rip took Sean's cell phone battery out and zipped it into his pack. It already held Gale's iPhone and his satphone. Not far from Peaks of Otter, an oncoming car flashed its lights.

"Pull over, *now!*" Rip shouted.

Gale and Rip ran into the woods. Around the next bend, Park Rangers waved Sean into a roadblock. They checked his driver's license and glanced in the car. An FBI agent would have recorded his name and crosschecked it against the ones from the camp, and the computer would have made the connection between Sean and Josh Stadler in seconds. But the rangers who had been ordered to hastily set up the roadblock were still waiting for the FBI to show up with more instructions.

They knew this gangly college student in an old Jeep didn't match the description of a mid-thirties or mid-forties couple they were given, so they let him pass.

13

Sean drove extra slow. Several cars passed him. A half-mile ahead, he pulled over at a trailhead and waited. Rip emerged cautiously from the woods. After making eye contact and getting a thumbs-up from Sean, he went back for Gale. They made Roanoke minutes before officials set up another checkpoint.

The Blue Ridge Parkway wound along the peaks and cliffs three to four-thousand feet above picturesque valleys, but Gale and Rip missed it all. They were asleep before the Jeep left Virginia. Five hours later, Rip awoke disoriented.

"We're in North Carolina, but still about sixty miles from Asheville," Sean said, switching hands on the wheel. "Should we stay on the Parkway? There's been no sign of trouble." Their voices woke Gale.

"Let's stay the course. Pull over the next chance you get and I'll drive." Rip checked his watch. At their current speed, it would be sometime around six p.m. when they got to Asheville. Rip wanted to find a phone, and he and Gale were very hungry. Trail mix, carrots, celery, and energy bars had sustained them for more than twenty-four hours. Food is somewhat scarce on the Parkway, but they were near Crabtree Meadows, a trailhead to

Crabtree Falls, with a rustic restaurant and country gas station. As a precaution, they parked between two large RVs. Rip kept his pack with him. They ordered food to go.

The waitress shook her head. "You folks just relax, things are slower here in the mountains," she said in a southern drawl.

Gale paid the bill, Sean got gas, and Rip placed a call from an old payphone. Sean insisted on driving the rest of the way, said he didn't like anyone else driving his "luxury ride." He wondered how long they'd be gone, and wanted to call his girlfriend, but thought it might be a dumb idea.

"I phoned an old friend in Pennsylvania," Rip said, explaining his ploy, "and asked him to drive to a payphone. He's going to call Larsen and tell him we're okay. He'll give Larsen a message that we're in Erie, Pennsylvania." He glanced over at Gale for effect. "Then he'll say that we've got a friend who will help us get across the lake and we'll be in touch once we're in Canada."

The Parkway reminded Gale of the country roads in Vermont where she grew up. Her youth held the seeds for why she had volunteered to become a fugitive. Feeling a constant pressure to create, she found writing to be a way to search for a lost understanding that haunted her, something that could explain what it all meant. She always sensed there was one piece of her life's puzzle missing. Early on, she developed an interest in theology, then esoteric concepts and non-religious spiritual philosophies. As an adult, she knew they were an attempt to fill that void, but it only seemed to clarify the absence of something more.

But when they pulled the globe from that cliff and she saw it light up, a surge of emotions overwhelmed her. It all seemed familiar, the Eysen, Rip, even the carvings and the gold bands on the Odeon. She couldn't explain it, not even to herself. When they heard people were coming after them to get the artifacts, it didn't surprise her. She'd been almost expecting it, at least subconsciously. She didn't know why, didn't know what the discovery meant, but she was sure that following Rip and protecting the ancient treasures was something she had to do.

There were more than a hundred men in the woods. Dogs picked up the scent and followed it to Indian Rocks. It was lost again at a nearby storage shed, but they had tire tracks. At the same time, an agent phoned Barbeau from Lynchburg. Sean Stadler owned a 1987 red Jeep Wrangler. The tires matched. Barbeau called off the foot-search.

"They're in that Jeep. Get the word out." He told a subordinate the plate number and then found Hall. "Let's get back to Washington. The Director wants a meeting."

Hall put an agent in charge. The camp would be kept secure, government research would continue, but he did not expect to return. On the helicopter flight, Hall studied photos of Gaines and Asher on his computer. He believed the face of the accused held more clues than the crime scene.

Leary and Nanski were in Warrenton, forty-five minutes into their trip, when they heard from Pisano. They turned onto US-17 and drove in the opposite direction from the mountains. They could be in Fredericksburg in just under an hour. With confirmation that the targets were in a vehicle, the search broadened. While waiting for the next break, Pisano wanted them to have a chat with Josh Stadler, who had seen the casing, knew what it contained, and had photos.

Larsen looked at his phone. "Restricted?" He answered. The caller identified himself as a friend of Rip's. Larsen pulled into a convenience store parking lot and listened.

He thanked the caller, relieved to hear they were safe and nearly to Canada. Larsen wanted to relay the news to Josh, but decided to wait until they met. He'd be in Fredericksburg in about an hour.

Barbeau and Hall were just arriving at the J. Edgar Hoover Building when they got word of an intercepted call. They now had two important leads. Sean Stadler, and Pennsylvania. Barbeau ordered a manpower shift and notified the Canadians.

"Looks like your brilliant Dr. Gaines has made a major mistake," Barbeau said.

"We don't have him yet."

"What is your problem Hall? Do you *want* him to get away?"

"Of course not, but we're missing something."

"That's why it's called an investigation, and we're the Federal Bureau of Investigation because we *investigate*. We'll find what we're missing soon enough, but first it's nice to apprehend the damn suspects so they don't do more bad things that we have to investigate."

A secretary escorted them to the office of the Director, who introduced them to his boss, Attorney General Dover. Barbeau briefed the country's top two law enforcement officials on the latest developments. The Pittsburgh field office would become the new command center.

"This is a huge case," Dover told him. "Tell the Director if you need anything. And bring them in."

Immediately after the meeting, Hall and Barbeau flew to Pennsylvania. Barbeau felt optimistic that they would have Gaines soon, but he also knew that each passing hour increased the likelihood that Gaines could slip away and force a protracted search. The memories of the five-year hunt for Eric Rudolph still haunted him.

14

Josh lived in a small ranch house at the end of a cul-de-sac. He usually spent only six to eight days a month there, depending on assignments. The FBI was spread thin on this case, and had asked for help from the Virginia State Police. The trooper assigned to watch Josh's house still hadn't shown up.

Josh arrived home around seven p.m. Exhausted, he left his camera bag on the hall table and headed to the kitchen, where a west-facing window caught the evening sun, washing the room in glaring light.

A smiling man, sitting at the kitchen table, startled him. Instinctively, he turned to escape and ran into Leary's solid frame.

"What is this?" Josh demanded.

Leary pushed him roughly toward the table.

"Please, Mr. Stadler," Nanski said. "We just have a few questions."

Josh grabbed a chair and swung it at Leary, who let out a grunt as it connected with his upper arm. Nanski grabbed Josh while Leary pulled out his 9mm Ruger, and in one swift motion pressed it to Josh's head. "Want to meet Jesus?" Leary whispered so softly that Josh wasn't sure he heard it.

"Mr. Stadler, this isn't necessary. We're only here to talk," Nanski said. "Now, are you going to cooperate?"

Other than those simple arrests during war protests, he'd never been this close to a gun. *These guys might kill me.* "Who are you? What do you want?" Josh asked in a trembling voice, still not realizing they had anything to do with the globe.

"We just want to ask you a few questions," Nanski repeated.

"Show me some identification then."

Leary smiled and moved the gun to Josh's face.

"I think my colleague has just shown you our ID," Nanski said. "Now, please tell us about the casing."

"I-I don't know what you're talking about," Josh stammered. "I want to talk to an attorney."

"Josh, we know you stole the casing from federal land and took it to the lab in Bethesda. We know you're helping the fugitives Professor Gaines and Gale Asher," Nanski said, taking out a stiletto knife that opened with a loud click.

Josh wondered if they were with the government. How else could they know this much? "I have nothing to say. I know my rights. Take me in."

Leary laughed.

"Listen, Stadler." Nanski's voice was now tense. "We're not taking you anywhere. You're going to tell us all we need to know right now."

Leary smashed the barrel of the pistol across Josh's face hard, knocking him to the floor.

They pulled Josh to his feet, then slammed him back in the chair. "You have no rights!" Nanski sneered from gritted teeth.

Josh's cheek burned as he felt the warm blood run down.

"Josh, we already have Sean. We picked him up early this afternoon. But he wasn't with the professor and Ms. Asher anymore. They are the ones we really want," Nanski explained as he carefully dabbed away the blood, acting concerned.

"What have you done with Sean?" Josh screamed at Nanski,

unable to see his features, backlit from the window. *These bastards can't be with the government.*

"Your brother is not in a condition to do much talking right now," Nanski said. "Don't worry, you'll see him. But first, tell us everything you know about the casing and what was inside of it."

"If you've hurt my brother—"

"Tell us about the casing," Nanski said, pressing the point of the stiletto against the cut in Josh's cheek, moving slowly up toward his eye. "Have you talked to anyone other than Sweedler at the lab? Who else have you told about the artifacts that Gaines found in the mountains?"

"No one."

"Are you sure?"

"I'm telling the truth."

"We have ways of confirming that," Nanski said, smiling. "Where is your camera?"

"In the hall," he answered and started to stand up, but Nanski pressed the blade deeper into his cheek, stopping him. He nodded to Leary, who moved toward the hall.

"Where is the other half of the casing?" Nanski asked, still smiling.

While Leary was gone, Josh's mind raced. He jerked his head away from the knife and kicked wildly, striking Nanski in the groin. The blow stunned Nanski. He dropped the stiletto and grabbed his crotch. Josh bolted into the living room. Leary grabbed him from behind just as he reached the sliding door leading to the backyard. Josh tried to elbow him, but Leary was quicker than he looked and threw his massive arm around Josh's neck. They fell to the carpet. Josh kicked and clawed as they wrestled.

"Move and you're dead!" Nanski shouted, one hand protecting his privates, the other pointing a .44 Magnum at Josh.

Leary got to his feet, wiped the bloody scratch on his face, tucked in his shirt, then kicked Josh in the back. Nanski held his gun steady a few feet away, never taking his eyes off the two men.

"Talk!" Nanski barked.

Josh could barely get the words out. "I've told you. I don't know anything about the casing. They asked me to take it to the lab and I did. That's it. I don't know where they are."

Nanski looked at Leary. He nodded and went back to the kitchen.

"That's not good enough. We're going to have to know for sure," Nanski said. "Now get on that couch. You can take a special chemical that will prove if you're lying."

"Forget it," Josh argued.

"Then my colleague is going to have to beat it out of you," Nanski growled.

Leary returned with a small vial of liquid. "It doesn't even taste bad, but we'll know if you're telling us the truth," Nanski said, smiling. "The magic of sodium-pentothal." He handed it to Josh. "Drink."

"No."

Leary slapped his wounded cheek.

"Then we'll do it the hard way," Nanski said, nodding to Leary.

"Wait!"

Josh, a gentle soul, deciding he didn't know enough to hurt Gale and Rip, drank the potion. For twenty minutes they questioned him aggressively until Josh's heart stopped. Of course, it hadn't truly been truth serum.

They didn't want him to tell the truth though. They wanted him silent forever.

15

Larsen had been to Josh's on plenty of occasions, but a major accident near Culpeper made him late this time. A tractor-trailer had swerved to avoid a steel girder in the middle of the road, slid off the pavement, taking two other cars with it, and overturned. Another few feet, another half-second, and Larsen might have been seriously injured. Instead, he pulled over, ready to help. Before his call to 911 went through, he saw two county sheriff's cars pull over on the westbound lanes. Somewhat shaken, Larsen headed east again, but unknowingly without his FBI trail since the agents had been caught behind the crash.

Larsen banged on the front door of Josh's house.

"Something's wrong with Josh," Nanski said as he opened the door and waved him inside.

Larsen ran, unthinking, into the house, "Is he hurt?"

"Down there," Nanski pointed.

Larsen entered the living room and saw Josh slumped over on the couch. Leary stood nearby pointing a gun at Larsen. "The Lord is having a long talk with your friend." He paused, smirking. "It's for the best. He sinned a lot." Leary bowed his head slightly.

Without hesitating, Larsen launched himself into Leary's

midsection. They tumbled against the wall. Larsen smashed his massive right fist into Leary's face, cracking his nose, spewing blood. He struck again before Nanski pulled him off, but Larsen kept the momentum going, pushing Nanski backward and pinning him against the couch.

Leary wailed, his face covered in blood. Clearing an eye, he scanned the room for his pistol. Larsen spun on Nanski, pulled him over, and shoved him into an end table. A heavy book fell off. Larsen scooped it up and sent it sailing into Leary's head, just as he reached for the gun. Nanski raised up and Larsen connected a heavy kick to his chest before fleeing the room.

He got through the front door and inside his car before Leary stumbled out of the house waving his Ruger. Larsen held down the car horn and floored the accelerator in reverse. Nanski pulled Leary back inside as Larsen squealed up the street.

The two men quickly, but expertly, put the house back together and left with Josh's camera case. It wouldn't be long before they would be able to catch up with Larsen again. Nanski drove Leary to the hospital and phoned Pisano from the waiting room. He reported that Josh was no longer a threat, and Larsen would not get away again.

Larsen headed south on Interstate 95 and pulled off at the first rest stop, the salty taste of tears on his lips. He jerked the car into an end space, opened his door, and rolled onto the pavement. He crouched there crying. His hands and legs ached. Questions tore through his mind.

Oh God, what did they do to poor, sweet Josh? Who were they? They weren't with the FBI. Does the government really have a secret police force that doesn't care about the Constitution? Or maybe someone else was involved?

Had Rip made it to Canada? Would he be safe there?

Larsen pulled himself together, got back in his car, and continued to search for answers as he drove farther south and deeper into the night.

Rip looked at his watch. Before fleeing the camp, Larsen and he had made a hasty plan to check in with each other once a day through an old girlfriend of Larsen's. He found a gas station on the edge of Asheville, thankfully one with a working payphone. Rip expected just to leave a message, but the girl told him Larsen had called an hour earlier. She gave Rip the phone number of a motel room.

Larsen answered on the first ring.

"Are you okay?" Rip hardly recognized his strained voice.

Larsen sat on the floor between two double beds. "No, not at all."

"What is it?"

"They've killed Josh."

Rip's knees buckled. He braced himself against the wall.

"Did you hear me? Josh is *dead*. They *killed* him!"

"What do you mean? Why? Who? Who killed him? Are you sure?"

"Yes, I'm sure, I saw his body! They tried to kill me too!"

"Who?"

"I don't know—"

Rip interrupted. "Where are you? When did this happen?" He looked back at Sean sitting in the car. The impossible task of telling him his brother was dead made him sick.

"After the feds allowed me to leave camp, I got hold of Josh and we agreed to meet at his house in Fredericksburg. Oh my God... it's my fault."

"No," Rip said.

"No, it's *your* fault. You have no idea. The FBI is all over this. These two thugs knew my name and Josh's," Larsen's voice grew higher, "and they tried to *kill* me. What the hell is that thing we found!?"

Rip could hear the terror in Larsen's voice, but he couldn't grasp what his friend was saying. "Larsen, where are you now?"

"I'm on 95 south heading home. I don't know what to do."

"Listen to me. You need to get to Booker. This is way out of control. We made a monumental find, but I can't believe someone is willing to *kill* for it. How do they even know about it? Were they monitoring the dig for some reason? There has to be something more going on."

"Believe it. These guys will kill you. Turn yourself in to the FBI. End this before someone else gets hurt."

"It's wrong... something is very wrong." Rip didn't know what else to say. His hands were trembling, his throat dry.

"Wrong? Is that the best you've got? You stole an artifact and someone is dead!"

"Larsen, I know. Get to Booker."

"You can stop this Rip. You're right about something being wrong. You broke the law, breached professional protocol, and acted unethically. If you—"

"Do they kill people for those kinds of things? No, Larsen. You know this isn't a normal find. This is beyond the rules."

"Josh is dead because of you!"

"I know! I never should have asked him to take the casing. But I am *not* turning myself in until we know more about the Eysen. Damn it, Larsen, you know we *just* dug them out of the ground. How do they know already? Why do they want them so badly? All this proves is that I did the right thing by running."

"Tell that to Josh."

"I'm sorry about Josh."

"What would you have said if I were dead right now?"

"You're not."

"Those killers are after me."

"That's why you need to call Booker. He'll protect you." Rip gave him Booker's private number. "Tell him everything. But we need to get off. It's not safe to be on the phone any longer. The government is always listening."

"Screw Booker, I need to call the cops!"

"You can't."

"Why, Rip? Why are we suddenly criminals? It's just a damn artifact. I don't care how old it is!"

"It's not just an artifact," Rip said, trying to control his voice. "It's something far more important. Something beyond rare. Something never really seen before."

"What is it?"

"It's the truth."

"What does that even mean? I need to know what you know. You can't ask me to go through all this —and more— without knowing everything."

"Please, I can't do this on the phone. You know me. That has to be enough for now until I see you again. Until I can show you." Larsen didn't say anything for so long that Rip thought he'd lost the connection. "Hello?"

"I'll call Booker," Larsen said, defeated. "Josh didn't deserve to die over this." His voice cracked.

"We need time. Gale and I will make it to Canada by morning." Rip felt bad lying to his best friend, but for now everyone had to think Canada was his destination. "You get to Booker. He'll protect you. I'll be back in touch when I can."

Rip hung up but stood at the phone for several minutes trying to calm down. He couldn't stop shaking. He didn't want to tell Sean.

Cash and a fake name got them into a room with two double beds at a dive motel in a forgotten mountain town well off the Parkway. They ordered sushi from a nearby take-out place, and searched the TV news channels for any sign of themselves or the Virginia dig. The absolute absence of coverage relieved them, but at the same time left Rip uneasy.

He mostly fidgeted with his food, but let the others finish eating before breaking the news.

"Sean. I'm not sure how to say this... but I just found out that Josh has been killed."

Sean choked. "What?"

Gale looked disbelievingly at Rip.

"My friend Larsen found his body—"

"What? Wait. No. I don't believe my brother is dead!" Sean cried. "Why would anyone kill Josh?"

"I don't know why exactly, but the same men tried to kill Larsen."

"Was your friend with him? What happened?"

"I didn't get details. The men were looking for us."

"He's not dead. How do we know?" Sean said, eyes blurry. "I have to go to him."

For thirty minutes Rip pleaded with Sean not to go. In the end, he could not be swayed.

"I have to go."

"It's too dangerous," Gale cautioned. "Whoever killed Josh could kill you too."

"Maybe, but don't you see?" Sean wiped tears and looked at her. "Josh would come for me."

Gale knew that was true. Josh adored his brother. Sean had already put himself in jeopardy to help them this long. It might be best for him to get out now. Rip returned Sean's cell phone.

"Don't use your phone unless you want the feds to find you. And remember, they'll likely be watching your place. Here's a phone number to someone who can get a message to us." Rip handed him a scrap of paper with Booker's number.

"Don't worry. If I'm caught, I'll say you were heading to Canada."

The FBI found Josh's body at about the same time Sean got onto Interstate 81. With no sign of foul play – the place looked immaculate – the county medical examiner initially attributed the likely cause of death to heart failure. He noted that it seemed unusual for someone so young and with no history of heart disease to die that way, but God works in mysterious ways.

16

Rip took the bed closest to the door. He'd braced a chair under the knob minutes after Sean's departure. Gale turned off the lights and they lay there silently.

Josh's death had changed things. It contaminated the air, leaving it heavy, painful, and dangerous.

"We killed Josh," Gale said finally.

"No. Our actions may have set off a chain of events that resulted in his death, but—"

"Same thing."

"Damn it, Gale. I'm sorry, but we all make decisions in our lives. Josh could have said no. He didn't have to take the casing. I could just as easily say it's your fault. If you and he had done what I asked and left the dig site, he'd still be alive."

Rip instantly regretted the words.

"You're right. Sure. If I'd never met Josh, if his mother hadn't given birth to him, if you'd become a goddamned car salesman!"

"That isn't what I meant to say. It isn't your fault. It's true that if I hadn't run off with the artifacts Josh would still be alive, but we're here now, and the important point is who killed him, and why."

"What do we have that is so valuable that someone would kill a photographer for it?" Gale asked.

"And how did they know about it so quickly? The FBI came to the camp too soon."

"How could it be that old?" Gale asked quietly, almost to herself.

"In the end, even if it's a thousand years old, the Eysen is earth-shattering." Guilt-ridden and stressed, he looked at her questioningly. "Do the FBI's tactics involve murdering material witnesses to what should be considered a minor theft? I doubt it."

"It doesn't make sense."

"They apparently don't believe anything about the artifacts is minor. Even so, there must be someone else involved. The FBI released Josh and Larsen. You're right. It doesn't make sense that they'd want to kill them twenty-four hours later."

"Damn it. What *is* the Eysen?" Gale demanded.

"I hope to begin to find out tomorrow. If we can stop running long enough and the sun can turn it on again."

Thursday July 13th

In the morning, while Gale slept, Rip studied the casing and the amazing array of circles and lines. Every way he looked at it he saw patterns – random and sequenced – and knew it held a message, or maybe many. But it would take time to figure it out.

Protect the artifacts, figure out their age, discover the secrets they contain, he thought to himself. *Then what? Is what the Eysen has to teach us something we're ready for? I need time. Hopefully Asheville will give me time . . . and answers.*

Gale awoke and silently watched him trace the carvings with his fingers, eyes transfixed. The brilliant archaeologist-fugitive she'd tied her fate to seemed overwhelmed in that moment. Following him was likely to be the biggest mistake of her life, but for the first time ever, she felt a purpose and a destiny at work.

After a quick breakfast at a nearby diner, Gale took a walk in a grove of trees beside the motel. She whispered an apology to Josh and asked him to help Sean. Rip had found a payphone in front of a nearby Laundromat and placed a collect call to Booker.

Booker, an only child born to an African-American father and a Caucasian mother, had been devastated at age nine by the death of his father. The family lost its home in an affluent Philadelphia suburb, and for several years bounced around low-end rental units until his mother passed her real estate exam.

At ten, Booker began buying collectibles at garage sales and reselling them to antique shops, through classified ads, or to a growing list of clients. If he found a Tiffany lamp, he learned all there was to know about them. *"Knowledge is power,"* his motto even then. He dropped out of school a couple of years later, saying he didn't have time *"for fill-in-the-blank busy-work and soda-pop history."* By thirteen he was submitting materials to auction houses. He bought and sold almost anything except drugs and guns. He told a friend once, *"They may be profitable, but the downside is so steep, you can't see up."*

Before turning eighteen, he had three full-time employees, paid under the table of course, and an army of part-time workers. He got into art as the market was getting hot and his cash piled up. Then he started buying real estate, using his mother as the exclusive broker. It wasn't long before Booker's companies filled an old ten-story downtown building. He played the stock options market, and by twenty-one was worth nineteen million officially, and twice that if the IRS wasn't looking. The press loved him, and he was a folk hero in the African-American community.

It was then that he got serious about money and began buying and selling companies. He was tough, made millions – tens of millions – and the media turned on him as he closed factories and sliced up businesses. The deals kept getting bigger though, and at thirty-five, *Forbes Magazine* estimated his net worth at $2.8 billion.

Booker was hated. Then the tech boom hit. He put his cash hoard into venture capital for dot-coms, made it out before the bubble burst, and by the time the second wave hit, he was sitting on more than $30 billion in assets. Many suspected his worth to be much higher. He retreated from public view, but his legend - like his power and wealth- continued to balloon. Although the public saw a ruthless tycoon, an air of mystery grew around him. There was another side to this complex individual.

It was that man who had phoned the young archaeology student years earlier. It was that man Ripley Gaines knew.

17

Booker made sure his line was scrambled, then paced to the window, his view that of crashing waves. "Damn it, Rip. You're lucky to be alive!"

"I know."

"Do you? The Vatican got Josh Stadler, and they mean the same fate for you."

"The Vatican? How the hell did *the Vatican* get into this?" Rip knew Booker had legions of valuable contacts around the world, but this information was unfathomable.

"Dover's got a direct line."

"The Attorney General?" He couldn't believe what he was hearing. "How did this get so big? How do *you* already know so much?"

"Dover is tight with the Vatican, and obviously Rome wants to cover this up. I suspect that anyone who knows anything is in danger, especially if they saw the artifacts."

"Booker, for all they know I just stole an ancient artifact from federal land."

"They know it's not an ordinary find. The Church has been on you since Cosega was published."

"Yeah, to kill *me*. But an innocent photographer?"

"Unfortunately, you've underestimated the importance people place on the acceptance of creationism."

"Creationism is a fairy tale! Evolution overthrew it decades ago."

"Not to the 1.2 billion Catholics in the world. Evolution just gave them something to fight against, but Darwin has too many holes to be a real threat. What *you* found might threaten the very foundations of the Church itself."

"The Church will find a way to dispute it."

"If you'd found a human skeleton that predates current thinking, that would be fairly easy to discredit. But you discovered intricate human carvings in eleven-million-year-old rock. Are the symbols a language?"

"I need time to study it." Rip's mind tried to process the information Booker had hit him with. "But it's much more than just the carvings. There is meaning."

"I assumed so, or the Vatican wouldn't be on the warpath."

"The Vatican," Rip repeated. Old fears twisted inside him. "How do they know already?"

"They are connected to everything."

"I know the Catholic Church has been the most influential force in the western world for more than a thousand years and they've gotten very good at concealing their power during the last century, but to exercise control over the US Attorney General and to kill people to stop word getting out . . . "

"You've spent your entire career looking for proof that humans predate creationism *and* evolution. The Church doesn't like that."

Rip looked around as a young couple exited the Laundromat, suddenly worried that anyone might be a Vatican agent. "How many will the Church kill to suppress this find? We are *not* living in the goddamned Middle Ages!"

"The Vatican may be the most powerful institution on the planet. Why do you think the feds are coming on so strong? If you'd run off with an old Indian burial mask the FBI would send one agent out of Oklahoma to work the case. If you have any doubt, just ask Josh Stadler."

Rip recalled the secrets from his youth. Because of them, he'd always feared the Church would come for him. He considered telling Booker the whole story, but quickly pushed the thoughts back into the past.

"Can you help us disappear?" He watched Gale walk toward him from the motel, her hair still wet from a shower.

"Of course," Booker said. "I've got too much invested to let the Pope get you. Larsen called in already. One of my people is on the way to his house in Florida. We'll keep him safe. In the meantime, I'll arrange a rental car for you and Kruse, one of my best guys who's close by. He'll meet you."

"Thanks Booker. I'll never know why you've done so much for me over the years, but I'm grateful," Rip said. "I just need time to figure all this out."

"Time's a funny thing. It might not be there when you need it," Booker said before ending the call.

Booker held business interests all over the world. For years he'd employed investigators to probe every aspect of a takeover target's operations, including the lives of its officers. There were people on his staff whose only job was to get hired by a company he was interested in buying or a competitor he wanted to destroy. He played hardball with organized crime, crossed every line in business, pushed, bribed, and eluded federal agencies. His contacts were everywhere. Along the way, he recruited and trained a smart and loyal army of agents for his security force, known as "AX." No one knew what AX stood for, but they knew the meaning. Its agents handled everything, from simple firings that turned ugly, to protecting executives in trouble spots. While the majority of AX agents worked in corporate espionage, some did more "controversial" work. One of Booker's best AX agents was a man known simply as Kruse, based in Knoxville, Tennessee.

Kruse, a weapons expert, had worked for Booker for almost a decade. His title – "Director of Research for the Southeast region of Boardwalk, Inc." – didn't really match his duties. Boardwalk – a product development company ultimately owned by Booker – actually served as a corporate espionage network with offices throughout the world. Kruse had been on standby for the Gaines assignment, but was surprised when Booker told him that nothing was more important to the billionaire.

18

The rental-car employee picked them up at the motel. After dropping the driver at his office, they stopped at an Asheville health food store. Gale picked up groceries while Rip waited in the car out of sight.

About thirty miles outside of town, Rip slowed down on the narrow country road. There was hardly a visible entrance, simply an eight-foot break in a mature hedge. A long gravel drive, bordered on each side by sycamore trees, extended for half a mile. Long ago, the underbrush had encroached, leaving the trees to defend the lane. It ended at stone columns adorned with antique black iron gates. Rip used a key on the big rusty padlock. After a curve, Gale commented on a tiny stone building with an oxidized green copper roof. Rip told her it was the wellhouse. The view opened, and the drive circled the front of a large, well-maintained two-story, stone cottage. Ivy covered the north walls, and manicured boxwood the periphery.

"It's lovely, but are we safe here?" Gale asked.

"Other than my father, no one knows of my connection to it."

"Then who takes care of it?"

"It belongs to a cousin. It used to be my uncle's home. He

had the best gardener for years. Even after he died and they closed up this place, old Topper couldn't let it go. He's maybe seventy-five now, but I'll bet he shows up here once a week or so to keep it up." Rip smiled. "He's like a grandfather to me."

"Has it been in your family for generations?"

"No. My uncle bought it in the 80s. We spent summers here while I was growing up. My cousin and her husband live in London. He's a journalist with *The Guardian*."

They stopped in front of the small portico supported by four wooden columns, matching the shutters and door. No one knew where they were. It was peaceful, their first real chance to breathe.

"Looks like a decent hideout."

"Topper's is the closest house, a mile through those trees."

Gale looked toward the woods where he pointed and tried unsuccessfully to see Topper's house.

"There's a book in the library inside that has a lot of history of the place. Ancestors of the man who sold it to my uncle built it in the late 1790s, but originally there was a cabin here that predated the Revolutionary War," Rip said, clearly proud of the historic home.

They approached the house. On the edge of the woods, behind a small iron fence, seven or eight antique gravestones stood like old storybooks concealing exciting tales. Rip looked over at them and thought of Josh, feeling responsible for his death and considering how well Gale seemed to be handling the loss of her friend. He walked toward the graves, absorbed in his own guilt. She followed.

She read the stones out loud. Some dates were barely visible. The earliest, 1743-1774, belonged to Elizabeth, no last name. She found that odd. For an archaeologist, those years were almost yesterday, but so much had changed in the two-hundred-seventy-some-odd years since Elizabeth had been born. Instead, he considered the events prior to her life: the first permanent settlement of whites a few hundred miles northeast at Jamestown in 1607, and before that the continent belonged to the Native Americans. They roamed for thousands of years, living in harmony with nature. An easier time. Fewer people, a practically endless expanse of land, and an abundance of game.

He thought of ancient ancestors walking across the Bering Strait, Africa's early humans, Neanderthals, and all the space between the time when someone placed the Eysen inside the stone casings and then it became buried in the cliff. What civilization could have created such objects to last and light up after millions of years? The constant running left no time to explore the extraordinary artifact in his pack.

Gale circled a pair of graves, the dates 1863 and 1864. "Brothers?" she asked.

"Civil War took them. It wiped out an entire generation," he said. "War, killing . . . all of human history is soaked in blood and violence, and for at least two thousand years religion has been at the heart of it all." He shook his head and motioned to the house. "We need to look at the Eysen. There may not be much time."

As they headed toward the house, he thought about telling her of the Vatican connection. She deserved to know. Her life was in danger too. Rip considered the fortitude Gale had already exhibited and wondered from where it had come. He would soon rely on her strength even more.

While waiting for Leary at the hospital, Nanski slipped a card-reader into his laptop. He'd found a memory card in a hidden pocket under a false bottom in Josh Stadler's camera case. Knowing Stadler's history, Nanski assumed it had been used to get photos out of unfriendly countries. Even before he inserted the card he knew the FBI didn't have these. It was immediately clear that these were photos taken after the ones of the cliff and the casing. There were about a dozen shots of the casing, similar to the images he'd already seen.

"What horror did all those carved circles promise?"

Then he saw the Eysen.

"*Phialam insignem lapidem ponetis*," he whispered to himself. *It's an evil-looking black ball*, he thought with dread.

Next he saw the glowing lights from inside.

"Dear God." His eyes closed. "Malachy knew. *Stone bowls bearing carvings*. Two bowls together hold the secret that will end the Church." It was the apocalyptic prophecy of the *Ater Dies*. "It is real, and Gaines has found it."

What Gaines had dubbed the Eysen, the Church had for centuries secretly referred to as the "*Ater Dies*," Latin for "Black Day."

This was way beyond Pisano. Nanski kissed his Saint Christopher medal and dialed a phone number in the Vatican he'd been given years earlier, but had never used.

A cardinal answered in Italian.

"It has come to this."

19

"We've got more than seventy federal agents and hundreds more state and local officers, and we've not found one solid trace of an egghead and a ditsy nature writer!" Barbeau yelled at Hall as they drove to the federal building in Erie. "We started with two good witnesses. Now the photographer is dead and we've lost Larsen Fretwell!"

"I guess we should have held them." Hall couldn't help but second-guess Barbeau's strategy.

"If we had kept them in custody we wouldn't know that Gaines is coming to Pennsylvania!" Barbeau blasted. Most of their resources were now concentrated in the northwestern portion of that state. A few other agents would be in Florida to pick up Larsen again if he tried to go home.

Hall's ringing phone interrupted their frustrating conversation. It was a quick call.

"Ian Sweedler is missing," Hall reported.

"Sweedler? The lab rat?" Barbeau asked.

"Right. An associate of Gaines. Stadler took the casing to him for dating. His wife reported him missing a few hours ago."

"Think he ran?"

"The local PD doesn't think so, and neither does our agent down there."

"Incredible!" Barbeau hit his hand with his fist. "We're missing something Hall. There's something about this case that's wrong. If we find that invisible element, we'll find Gaines."

Nanski and Leary chartered a flight out of Richmond to Erie, Pennsylvania. Leary, with bruises, two cracked ribs, and a broken nose, had been hoping to catch up to Larsen, but Pisano sent someone else to Florida to wait for him there. Their mission differed from the feds' in one important way.

Although both groups were trying to retrieve the artifacts, the feds planned to arrest all those involved. The Church needed anyone who had seen the artifacts dead.

Nanski had clear instructions and a promise of unlimited resources. The challenge was not to broaden the mission to the point where it spun out of control. The Church needed the Eysen, needed it before anyone else learned of its existence. Nanski didn't even tell Leary about it. The casing was enough. Still, he worried. Secrets this dangerous were nearly always impossible to keep.

Sean drove all night except for a quick two-hour nap around four a.m., and made it to his brother's house just past nine in the morning. He found the hidden key by the front door. The state police officer assigned to watch the house stopped sipping coffee from a thermos. The Jeep was the wrong color. They'd been looking for red, but primer grey was easy enough to cover. The plates matched, and even from a distance Sean fit the description. *This is it,* he thought. The trooper radioed for back-up as he watched the suspected terrorist enter the house.

Sean found no trace of his brother, but he did notice the house seemed neater than usual. Maybe now he should call his girlfriend. She was smart- way smarter than him- but did he want to involve her? He sat on the couch to think and almost immediately nodded off.

The ringing phone jarred him. Hoping it might be Josh, he ran to the kitchen and answered it.

"Sean, there's an undercover cop watching the house. More are on the way to arrest you. Get out of there now. Leave from the back door. You'll never get away in your Jeep."

"Who is this?"

"A friend of Rip's. Hurry!" the man shouted, "Get out now!" Then he hung up. Booker's agents, parked nearly a block behind the state trooper, watched the house through binoculars, and saw a front shade move ever so slightly. Moments later, Sean sprinted through a small strip of trees that separated Josh's house from another neighborhood. By the time the SWAT van pulled up ten minutes later, he had put a mile between himself and the house.

Gale gazed at the books covering the walls from floor to ceiling. Glass doors enclosed the shelves on the south wall, protecting the oldest volumes. A tall window in the middle provided light as well as a view of the lawn and a small pond with an arched bridge to a tiny island the size of a king-sized bed. She settled into the wide window seat on an old faded leather cushion and turned to take in the room while waiting for Rip.

His uncle had purchased the house furnished with the books included, many of which went back to the original occupants. Gale replaced the volume she was looking at, an 1814 edition of *The Pilgrim's Progress* by John Bunyan, and was moving across the well-worn Oriental rug when Rip entered.

He placed his pack on the long, narrow library table, and,

with a chance to study what they'd risked so much to protect, pulled out half the casing again. He'd learned from Booker that the other half was now in the hands of the FBI, or worse, the Vatican. Gazing at the incredible object felt overpowering.

"Not only does this one object singlehandedly prove my Cosega Theory," Rip began, "it dramatically alters the Earth's history."

He didn't need Sweedler to tell him it had been buried for eleven million years. No other explanation made sense. But he knew that the date of origin would eventually need to be proven in order to satisfy the scientific community.

Will I ever get that chance? he wondered.

"If this is as old as that cliff, doesn't it actually change our place in the universe?" Gale asked.

"I couldn't argue with that statement."

His entire career, exploring ancient layers of earth all over the planet, had not prepared him. This wasn't just another stone artifact of a sophisticated society that had survived millennia. It wasn't just the missing link of evolution. In fact, it wasn't just proof of the Cosega Theory. The casings and the Eysen made them all, and every other fact of science, history, or religion, a lie.

"I can't believe someone carved these symbols eleven million years ago," Gale said, rubbing her hand over the intricate circles and lines. "I mean, my mind can't even *fathom* one million years."

"A few years back I worked with a team in Australia researching the oldest known piece of earth. It was a tiny speck of zircon crystal 4.4 billion years old. I was in awe of the incomprehensible age of the thing, but that was the universe at work. This casing was done by human hands." He pulled his laptop out of the pack and plugged it in. "Everything society believes today tells us that this casing would have been carved by apes eleven million years ago. Modern man didn't exist yet!"

As spectacular as the casing was, it paled next to the Eysen with its highly polished black metallic look and eerie glow. He set the Eysen atop a pillow in the center of the table, next to the casing and the Odeon. During his career, he'd seen nearly every substantial artifact from history's grandest civilizations that archaeology had uncovered, but all of them combined did not come close to the beauty, mystery, or impact of the three objects before him.

Rip realized he'd been holding his breath and finally exhaled. He and Gale fell into a reverent silence, as if the whole world hushed while they took in the enormity of what they had.

Other than the three inlaid gold lines on each, the Odeon and the Eysen were featureless, unlike the ornate carvings in the casing. The Eysen possessed a depth though. The lights they'd seen a few days earlier divulged a deeper secret.

"Ready?" Rip looked at Gale. "Let's see what the sun shows us."

Leaving the casing behind, Gale carried the Odeon and Rip the Eysen to a small deck behind the house. They carefully put down the objects and waited.

20

Sean ran for four or five miles before slowing down. Within a couple of hours, he arrived at Jefferson Davis Highway and found the Greyhound station. Sweat dripped from his face when he reached the ticket counter. Forty minutes until the next bus for Virginia Beach. *I can do that*, he thought. He had just enough cash for the $46.50 ticket. If all went well, he'd be at his parents' oceanfront house at 68th and Atlantic Avenue by six p.m. This was something he needed to tell them in person. He dreaded his mother's reaction.

Two hours into Sean's trip, Barbeau, still in Erie, gave the order for the SWAT unit to storm Josh's house. The Virginia State Police had surrounded the house within six minutes of Sean's getaway. Half an hour later, the FBI showed up and negotiations began. For almost four hours they tried to raise their target with all methods available, Sean being too important to risk killing.

Barbeau didn't like the coincidence of Josh Stadler's death. It worried him that organized crime or someone else might be involved. He might be missing something big.

Sean could get him to Gale and Rip. The Jeep was already being printed and dissected. Barbeau, in constant contact with the field commander throughout the siege, finally ran out of patience. They were desperate to talk to Sean.

Snipers were in position on nearby roofs, TV film crews had tape rolling as tear gas canisters were shot into every window. Moments later, SWAT officers kicked in the front door and smashed the sliding glass door from the back. Barbeau waited on the line for almost eight minutes until he heard, "Negative, target is absent."

"What is this, the Keystone Cops?" he shouted into the phone.

Most of a day had been wasted on a major lead for nothing. How had Sean Stadler escaped? People would be suspended. There had also not been a single sighting of Gaines or Asher, in Pennsylvania or anywhere else, since they left the camp.

"All we've got is an empty get-away vehicle and an old bowl carved out of rock," Barbeau barked.

Hall just stared at a yearbook photo of Sean and muttered to himself, "This scrappy kid is going to give us a boatload of trouble."

Nanski and Leary got the report and were told to give Pennsylvania one more day, then return to Virginia to pick up Sean's trail.

"Sean Stadler is the best chance we have of finding the professor," Pisano told them.

The Fredericksburg standoff made the networks' national feeds, reporting that a suspected terrorist had eluded the FBI. However, law enforcement officials were refusing to release a name or a photo of the suspect, citing national security concerns. Nanski and Leary watched it on CNN, a typical story – all photos and fluff – short on facts.

Nothing happened for a long two minutes while Gale and Rip stood watching the artifacts. Then, suddenly, purple and yellow lights emanated from the otherwise solid black Eysen. While the Odeon appeared unchanged by the sun, the Eysen's light show continued to build. They moved back several feet to what they thought might be a safe distance.

"I wonder, I mean this . . . " Rip's words collapsed. He could not believe what he was seeing and kept looking away from the Eysen to the house, the trees, anything to maintain his grip on reality. A mystical event unfolded in front of them. Standing became a burden, and they sank to their knees.

The lights grew in brightness, and other colors appeared – violets, pinks, aquas, yellows, golds, etc. The colors formed circles, figure-eights, triangles, diamonds, then more complex patterns, faster and faster until they saw incredibly intricate geometric shapes. The lights merged until no black remained in the top half of the Eysen. Then, astonishingly, an image appeared.

"Oh, God, can you–? Are you seeing this? Gale, my God! I just . . . Can you see? It's a picture. It's showing us a picture," Rip laughed nervously.

Tears ran from Gale's eyes as she held her face. She opened her mouth to respond, but no sound would come. Then the image came into focus, the display showing perfect resolution, higher than any high-def they'd ever seen. In that absolute clarity, they saw the planet Earth.

Suddenly, they heard music, an opera, a tenor. They took their eyes off the Eysen for the first time and looked at each other in wonderment. For an instant, they thought the music was coming from the Eysen. Then it grew louder, coming from the trees – a man singing opera. Rip glanced back at the Eysen. The Earth image rotated slowly inside. He threw the shirt it had been wrapped in over it just as the man emerged from the woods singing the best-known aria from Puccini's *La Bohème*.

"Oh, Jesus, it's Topper." Rip exhaled. He realized he'd been terrified. They were wanted, federal fugitives. Josh had been murdered by someone, the same someone now pursuing them. In their possession, they had some kind of window into the past.

Rip's heart pounded.

Gale took his hand. "Your hands are ice-cold."

Topper waved when he saw them.

"I'll be right back." Rip ran the Eysen and the Odeon back into the house, stashing them in the backpack, which he stuffed in a library cabinet.

"I see you two have introduced yourselves," Rip said, returning outside and finding Gale and Topper in conversation on the deck.

Gale nodded. She still hadn't recovered from the Eysen.

Topper hugged Rip. "We just needed some R and R," Rip said, making quick eye contact with Gale to make sure she hadn't already said something else. "And we really don't want anyone to know we're out here."

"This is the place for all that." Topper winked and began to lead Gale toward the pond. "You know I carved that bridge. Did it maybe thirty, thirty-five years back. Ripley was just a little thing then, and his mother didn't want him crossin' that water on some ol' boards he'd laid out."

Gale looked back at Rip, hoping he had a plan to get rid of Topper so they could return to the Eysen. Rip, still dazed from the sight, shrugged and followed.

It was muggy, temperatures in the eighties, humidity even higher. The three of them slowly crossed the bridge and walked the property for more than an hour, talking about Rip's childhood. Once Topper discovered that Gale worked for *National Geographic*, he recounted many of his favorite issues, most from before she'd been born.

"Topper, it's been great seeing you," Rip finally hinted at a farewell.

"Oh," he looked hurt. "I guess I need to be gettin' back to tendin' my garden."

"But you'll join us for dinner tomorrow, won't you?" Gale asked, trying to repair his feelings.

"I'd like that, Miss," he said with a lingering stare. "Y'all watch the trees. Leaves are blowin' back. There's a storm coming up." The aria picked up again as Topper disappeared into the woods.

21

With Topper gone, Rip retrieved the Eysen. This time he yanked the umbrella out of the patio table and rested the Eysen in the hole. Gale brought out a big salad and sourdough bread. They pulled up chairs and watched as the sequence that had captivated them earlier as it repeated itself.

"Obviously, this thing is solar-powered," Gale said.

Rip, still feeling completely overwhelmed by the impossible experience, took notes. Once the earth began to rotate, they could see the planet looked different than the modern Earth they knew. From the vantage point of the North Pole, a smaller and more circular ice cap existed, and a striking difference could be seen in the continents. There seemed to be only two large land masses. They could pick out features from coastlines like Greenland and South America, but everything appeared closer together.

"Rip, these images are taken from above the planet, from space." The details of the features were almost identical to satellite photos.

He let out a long breath. "You're right. It's impossible."

"So either this belonged to an advanced civilization that trav-

eled into space, or someone brought it here from another planet," she reasoned.

The earth revolved inside the Eysen as they continued to
deliberate the implications of their discovery. At least ten
minutes went by before they realized that nothing new was
happening. The Earth was simply going round and round. They
studied the image, which appeared three-dimensional, and was
confined to the top half of the Eysen. The lower portion
remained black. Rip picked it up and the image portion shifted
so that it stayed on top no matter how he held it.

"It's like a needle on a compass, always pointing north," Gale
said.

"Like there's an outer skin or something," Rip added. Almost
immediately, the Earth stopped spinning and began getting
smaller. As it shrank, other planets came into view. First Mars,
and at almost the same time they noticed the moon revolving
around the Earth. The scale continued to shift. Venus and
Mercury came into view, then the Sun and the other planets in
the solar system. Rip moved the Eysen in his hands to get a
better angle and the image zoomed in onto the surface of Mars.
It showed far more detail than our current mappings of the
planet, and something else. Something extraordinary.

Green. There were large sections of green vegetation on
Mars!

"It must be heat-sensitive or something. I think my movements are causing the images to change," he said.

The Carolina sky grew darker as thunderheads moved in.
The imposing clouds quickly smothered the sun, but the Eysen
kept flashing images. Rip moved his hands and got pictures from
a jungle, an island during a volcanic eruption, and more planetary
tours. The Eysen seemed to be displaying the composition of a
large crater being analyzed when the first raindrops hit. The sky
suddenly opened into a deluge of rain and they reluctantly
dashed inside.

Even in the house, the images continued. A series of moving

pictures flashed, showing what appeared to be dwellings – round and perfectly smooth – almost matching the surrounding grounds and vegetation. They wanted desperately to see inside one of the structures, but as soon as Rip moved his hands, the image switched to a large shark swimming. He slid his fingers up the Eysen and the scene changed to a huge forest fire.

"It's like an interactive issue of *National Geographic*!" Gale exclaimed.

"Jesus, look at this," Rip said slowly. The screen now showed rows of symbols like those carved on the casing. "Gale, get the casing, quick." She ran to the library. "Never mind," he said deflated. "It's gone off again." They would have to wait until the sun returned in the morning.

"But we don't have to stop." Gale said. "Don't you see? The Eysen has stolen the show with its mysteries and lights, but it just showed us that the key may be hidden in the carvings of the casings."

"Maybe you're *not* just another annoying reporter," Rip said, reaching for the casing. "What do circles represent? I mean not just to us, but throughout nature, across time?"

"Infinity. The circle is a symbol of completeness. An unbroken line with no beginning and no end. There are those who see it as representing the divine, or God." She touched the casings lightly, tracing the patterns. "See these circles with the dots in the middle? That is an actual ancient symbol for the source, or God."

"You know a lot about symbols?"

"I believe there's more to the world than we can see, than we know."

"Are you religious?"

"I prefer the term 'spiritual'."

"Hmm. What else do circles mean? The sun, earth—"

"Other planets."

"The moon, Saturn's rings."

"Ripples from a pebble in a pond. Circles appear all

throughout nature. Flowers, oranges, rings of a tree, sand dollars, eyes – pupils and irises. I've even seen crop circles with some of these patterns."

"Crop circles? Great! Another reason for my peers to ridicule me," Rip said.

"I did a story on them. They're real."

"Sure, some can't be explained. But there have been enough that were hoaxes that mainstream science has all but given up on them."

"Yeah, feed us enough lies and we forget what's true. One day they'll deny the Eysen ever existed," she said.

Rip didn't respond.

"The circles look like orbits. Maybe planetary alignments," Gale suggested.

"Hmm. Are you into astrology, too?"

"The study and movement of heavenly bodies is *astronomy*, not astrology," she replied.

"The circles are a language. A message."

"How can you be so sure?"

"Because I've been looking for this thing for almost twenty-five years, and no one would put this much work into decorations. It has a purpose, and that is to preserve and convey information."

"Couldn't they just do that through the Eysen?"

"Maybe, but what if the Eysen didn't last? And, perhaps like you said, the casings are a key to unlocking the Eysen."

"But we only have one-half of the globe. Don't you think we need both casings?" Gale asked.

"We've got Josh's photos of the other half. Anyway, I'm almost certain it's related to the sequence we see when the Eysen starts up . . . the Cosega Sequence."

"It could take a lifetime to decode something like that."

"Depending on how long we can stay alive."

22

Sean jogged three blocks from the bus station to the beach, took off his shoes and socks, then walked in the surf for the final forty-three blocks of his journey home. Tourists still lingered on the beach, but many had moved into the seafood joints along the boardwalk.

It had been a few weeks since his parents had seen him, and they welcomed the surprise. The Stadlers were a close-knit family, and as soon as his mother saw his face she knew something was wrong. Sean looked awful, with dark circles under his eyes. They followed him out onto the deck overlooking the ocean. During the bus ride he'd debated where to tell them, not wanting to forever ruin their view of the Atlantic, but finally deciding that the ocean might help comfort them.

He started at the beginning of the story as he knew it. There was no other way.

Hours passed. The sky went turquoise and crimson as night came. The moon found itself on the black ocean. Tears mixed with sadness and rage. More hours went by, silence, and whispers. A pink band grew on the horizon where the ocean caressed the sky. Orange and gold as the sun rose from the sea. Only then did they sleep.

While the storm raged through the mountains of North Carolina, Rip worked. He wrote notes about the Eysen, trying to document all the images it had displayed and in what order, made measurements of the three artifacts, and typed theories and questions on his laptop. Finally, Gale coaxed him out of his den. They sat in front of the living room's picture window overlooking the pond and back lawn, watching lightning split the silver rain. They talked about the Eysen.

"Do you know there is a story that when the American Indians first saw Columbus in his ships approaching them, they could not see the ships?" Gale asked him.

"What do you mean?"

"All they saw were strange waves on the horizon. They had never seen a ship. So, they could not see it. After a while, a shaman trained himself to see the ships. He explained to the rest of the Indians that what they were looking at were not waves, and he described the ships to them. Then, they all saw the ships."

"I've never heard that before."

"Makes me wonder what other images were in the Eysen that we couldn't see. I mean, all we saw were things that were familiar to us. Maybe pictures of things we can't comprehend flashed, but we couldn't see them."

Rip already had a headache and this wasn't helping. He asked her if they could just sit quietly for a while. Soon the rain stopped, the lightning moved into the distance, and the sun found a few holes to shine through as it sank into the trees.

They fell asleep in the living room. Rip woke a short while later with a grinding headache. He questioned every action they had taken since finding the Eysen. The possibility that he'd made nothing but mistakes troubled him. Gale sat up and put her hands on his shoulders. She stared into his eyes. The blue engulfed him.

"Meditate," she whispered.

"I don't know how," he said, embarrassed. Not because he didn't know how, but because he didn't want to disappoint her. She had him move to the floor, crossed her legs, and pointed so that he would do likewise.

"Take a deep breath." He did and his eyes closed. "Keep your eyes open, Rip. Look into my eyes." His back felt warm, as if a soft heated blanket was draped around him. "Feel yourself breathe in slowly . . . now feel yourself breathe out slowly."

Already, the controlled breathing soothed him.

"From your stomach, low," she said. "Bring the breaths from deep within."

Josh and the Eysen swirled in his thoughts, the FBI and helicopters, back to Josh. His breathing quickened.

"Rip, just feel your breaths. Nothing else matters."

"It's not that easy."

"Look into my eyes. Take my hands." She moved her hands closer to him. Their knees were touching as they sat cross-legged, facing each other. He reached up and put his hands in hers.

"Focus on my pupils and try not to see anything past the irises." Her voice sounded like a lullaby.

The blue captured him again – a Caribbean lagoon reflecting sunlight off white sand and coral. He heard his breaths, which were suddenly as loud as if that were the only sound there was. The tension in his body melted. The out-breaths were longer than he ever knew possible. They carried off his fears.

23

Friday July 14th

Just after ten a.m., Larsen stopped at the Sand Bar Convenience-and-Souvenir shop about a mile from his house at Cape San Blas, Florida. He stared out at the ocean before he went in. It was good to be home.

He picked up some basics and planned to sleep on the beach for the rest of the day. The salt air and gulf breeze peeled back layers of stress and kept him in a fog of denial. Then, while retrieving his held-mail, he found himself chatting about local gossip with the part-time postmaster as if all the terrible things hadn't happened. Larsen drove the final eight blocks to his driveway.

As he walked through the front door, he almost tripped over a lawn chair with a note taped on it. Still standing in the front hall, he looked around nervously, then grabbed the note. He read it twice before shoving it in his pocket. Larsen tensed as he walked to his bedroom and stared, only for an instant, at the two men tied and gagged on his bed. One appeared dead. The other looked straight at him and tried to yell through the duct tape on his mouth.

Larsen quickly closed the door and dashed out the back. Once on the deck, he surveyed the scene – a few dozen sunbathers scattered up and down the beach, a group of teenagers wading a pair of mini-cat sailboats past the surf, and several couples walking the shoreline. Larsen's house sat on stilts and afforded a long view. The only danger appeared to be in his bedroom. He moved slowly down the steps to the dunes between him and the beach, looking suspiciously at everyone. He was terrified.

The note told him that one of the bound men had been sent to arrest him, the other to kill him. It finished with a clear warning: *"If you want to remain alive and free, leave the house immediately. Go to the pier, and a man in a green ball cap will find you and get you to safety."*

Larsen assumed the unsigned note had been left by one of Booker's people, but then wondered, *Is it safe to assume anything?*

Taking off his shoes and socks, he tried to look natural. It was roughly twenty-six blocks to the pier, and every step of the way he considered running in the opposite direction. He wanted out of the madness his life had become.

Larsen thought back to when Josh had visited the previous summer. The two of them went shark fishing at midnight off the end of the pier. They didn't catch anything, but a few of the old-timers around them had had better luck. Larsen didn't care though. It was more about the moon and stars caressing the ocean in that pale light that exists only on a hot summer night in Florida. They stayed out all night, sipping cold beer and listening to fishing stories in various southern accents, then they slept most of the next day on the beach.

Half way to the pier, he moved slowly away from the breaking waves and slipped into the white dunes, ignoring a sign promising all kinds of terrible fines and punishments if he walked on them. The wind-created dunes act as a buffer to protect coastal lands from salt intrusion and erosion. He needed

a concealed place to think, and he found a low spot ringed with
ten- to twenty-foot-high dunes topped with sea oats.

Since they found the Eysen, Larsen had known they were in
way over their heads.

In Erie, Barbeau studied maps of Virginia and Pennsylvania, not
looking for anything in particular, just trying to get a feel for
how his targets had slipped away. Barbeau loved maps, and he
pulled them out whenever he was stressed or upset. He could
just as easily be looking at one of Norway or Prague. Something
in the lines, how they defined borders, rivers, and roads was
appealing, orderly. He could see so much from above, and maps
gave him control.

He stared at the contours of the Jefferson National Forest,
approximately seven-hundred-thousand acres, but it abutted the
George Washington National Forest, which added another
million acres. The mountains were dense with pines, steep cliffs,
and tumbling waterfalls. "Hell, they could still be up in those
mountains!" he yelled, as Hall entered the room.

Hall looked at the map covered conference table and also
wondered how the fugitives had disappeared. "Why would they
still be there? What about the Jeep tracks near Indian Rocks?"
As soon as he mentioned the Jeep, he regretted it and quickly
tried to change the subject. "Let's get some people back in the
mountains if you think Gaines might still be around."

"Damn Sean Stadler!" Barbeau shouted. "We got the Jeep!
We know the tire tracks match, but even though we had his
dead brother's house surrounded, this dumb college kid just
walked away. Hell, Gaines is probably having a big party right
now. It could be in the lobby of the J. Edgar Hoover Building and
we still couldn't find him." He slapped his hand on the table.

Hall thought of volunteering to hike the Appalachian Trail,
willing to search for them himself just to get away from Barbeau.

"You said yourself they'll make a mistake. It's just a matter of time. We'll get them."

Larsen didn't know what to do. It might be a trap. Surely Booker wasn't crazy enough to have people assault federal agents. While Larsen contemplated his next move, a man walking the beach, listening to what appeared to be an MP3 player, began moving toward Larsen's house, entering it surreptitiously. A few minutes later the man, having untied his fellow agent, exited the house with him, leaving the other man tied up for later questioning.

Those two joined two other FBI agents already on the beach, all of them dressed as tourists. They were moving quickly in all directions. Larsen had no clue.

A stocky woman, standing near a neighboring house, watched the feds come down the stairs and assumed that Larsen must already be on the beach. She crushed her cigarette out in the sand, then scoured the beach, angry that she had missed him. Even in their shorts and colorful shirts, the FBI guys stuck out on the expansive beach.

Watching them fan out, she thought, *They don't have any idea where he is, but neither do I.* She'd memorized Larsen's face, but even without the photo, a guy standing six-foot-seven should be easy enough to spot on an open strip of sand. A pretty college girl playing guitar caught her eye, and not far from her she saw footprints leading into the dunes. Most folks respected the dunes, but maybe a scared man hadn't. She followed them.

Larsen moved toward the pier, weaving through dunes, sweating while debating each step. Twice cheating death in forty-eight hours left him edgy. Unbeknownst to him, someone was just thirty yards behind him and closing in.

At the same time, the two feds heading toward the pier caught the attention of Finn Lambert, Booker's man in the green ball cap, who was waiting for Larsen. A former agent himself,

Lambert spotted them right off. Instead of staying, he began walking to his car parked on a dirt side street leading to the pier.

The stocky woman caught up to Larsen in the dunes and drew her weapon. "Larsen Fretwell- stop where you are!" She shouted the order from less than ten feet away.

24

Rip awoke at dawn and, while Gale slept, he sat on the porch reflecting on the extraordinary week. He was about to get the Eysen when a cardinal interrupted his solitude, emerging from a nearby evergreen and flying close. Its bright red coloring told him it was a male.

He remembered a similar bird from childhood. He'd been eight years old, playing near the stream not far from the house when a cardinal had landed and looked directly at him. Back then he thought blue jays and cardinals were brothers and sisters. He fell back through memories to a day, three decades earlier, when as a young boy he'd whispered to a cardinal, and the path of his life forever changed.

"Pretty bird, pretty bird," he'd said. The cardinal moved its head in a circle. "Shh-oo-wee, shh-oo-wee," he hushed, just like Topper had taught him. The bird came closer, and young Rip reached for it. Amazingly the cardinal flew and flapped in front of his face like a hummingbird, then turned and glided toward the trees. Rip had followed as it led him into the woods. He pursued it farther into the forest than his uncle allowed; past the old tree fort, around the big rock outcropping, and across the ravine. All the while the bird stayed close, just out of reach. He slowed in the meadow, having never been beyond it. The bird teased in the wildflowers. The perfumed breeze of late spring in the mountains pushed him on as the bird fluttered toward the trees.

Young Rip followed the bird and was soon lost. Just as he realized he didn't know the way home, the cardinal landed on a high, stone wall.

"It's a castle!" he said out loud.

Even to a young boy, the tall structure seemed out of place. Hidden by the trees, and somehow majestic in its ruin. He went through the doorway and inspected his royal fortress. Imagining himself to be a prince, commanding armies of knights, protecting the town outside his palace, he climbed the walls and surveyed his kingdom.

The bird landed on a corner and perched there while Rip continued to explore. The four aging, roofless walls towered around the little boy. He wondered who built it, and why. How long had it been there?

Sunlight penetrated the treetops, creating a ballet of shimmering shadows and dappled light. He noticed a strange, chiseled name on a smooth section of stone: "Clastier." That, he decided, would be the name of his kingdom, and he would be forever known as Prince Ripley of Clastier.

Soon Rip grew tired and hungry. He looked around, but couldn't figure out which direction to go. The scared eight-year-old, too frightened to cry, was alone in the woods. Without the bird, everything seemed different, but he remembered that the sun was in his eyes for most of the journey to Clastier Castle. He walked with the sun at his back and eventually reached the ravine and the big rock outcropping. Once he saw the old fort, he started to laugh. Rip's first big adventure planted the seeds for all that came after.

Gale awoke thinking about the Eysen, let a hot shower wash away some of the stress, then found Rip on the porch.

"See that cardinal?" he asked her.

"Beautiful. My favorite bird," she said.

"Really? It's because of a cardinal just like that one that I became an archaeologist."

"Then we're in this mess because of a bird? Maybe they're not my favorite anymore."

He proceeded to tell her the story of Clastier Castle.

"Take me there."

"We need to study the Eysen."

"Bring it. I've got almond scones and I'll grab a thermos of hot tea." She smiled.

"Tempting."

"Come on Rip, we need to breathe. I'll throw in some apples."

But it was her twinkling eyes that made him change his mind.

While walking through the forest, their conversation centered mostly on what they were going to do next. Although they felt safe in Asheville, staying anywhere too long was not wise. They needed time to study, time to think. But with the forces aligned against them, Rip knew there was perhaps only one person powerful enough to ensure their escape and provide a place to hide – Booker.

"Wow," Gale said as they reached the castle. "I can't imagine discovering this place as a kid. No wonder you became an archaeologist."

"It's been thirty years since that day with the cardinal . . . I've changed a lot since then, yet this place has stayed the same," Rip said.

"You like that, don't you?"

"Yeah. I love that about archaeology. The world keeps going after someone dies. Even an entire civilization can end and the world keeps moving ahead – changing. Yet, all these clues are left behind – unchanged."

"Like windows into the past."

"Exactly."

"Did you come back here a lot after that first visit?"

"I'll say. This old castle became the centerpiece of my childhood summers."

"It's magnificent."

"You wouldn't know it now, but I cleaned and cleared it. Man, I investigated every possible nook, made up endless stories about its origin and purpose."

Rip silently recalled that after Clastier Castle, every old building he encountered stirred his interest. But Clastier cemented Rip's future for another reason. One hot day during the summer he was sixteen. Ever since that particular day, he'd been searching- and fearing- the Catholic Church.

Gale wandered around the perimeter, running her fingers along the walls of beige, gray, and white stones. The structure must have been eighty feet long and half as wide. The odd part about the ruin was that the walls went up in varying heights, some parts as high as nine feet, but there were no other stones around the area. "Where are all the missing stones?" Gale asked.

"Often when a building goes down, the stones are quarried for another structure."

"Your uncle's house?"

He nodded and followed her through the main doorway, now covered in grass and underbrush.

"It looks like it might have been a big church or a giant warehouse," Gale said.

"As a kid, to me it was a castle, but you're right. It was a church," Rip said, not wanting to get into what he had learned during the intervening years. Two mature oak trees occupied the better part of the interior, and several smaller varieties were attempting to join the congregation.

"It looks like there may have been a fire," Gale said, pointing at the blackened higher stones.

"The building probably dates to around 1750 or so," Rip said, ignoring her guess.

"Enough of that," Gale said, sitting on a window ledge. "Will you meditate with me again?"

"What, here?"

"Yes. There's no better place than nature to connect with yourself." She smiled. "No distractions, no pressures."

"No distractions, no pressures? Have you forgotten that the FBI, and who knows who else, are after us?"

"Clear your mind, Rip. It will help you make better decisions, and maybe to *see* differently into the Eysen."

"Gale, there's something else I've been wanting to tell you, and strangely, this old ruined church seems an appropriate place."

Gale's concern grew as Rip's face became strained again.

He moved over and leaned against a tree nearer to her. She couldn't imagine how this situation could get any worse or more complicated.

"What is it?" Gale asked while trying to find his eyes. They were following a squirrel skittering across the top of the south wall and onto an overhanging branch.

"It's pretty serious." He returned her stare. "I know who killed Josh."

Her eyes squinted in a pained expression. The intensity of her visible emotion moved him. "Who?"

"Agents for the Vatican killed him."

She looked at him disbelievingly. "The Vatican has *agents*? Who *kill*? How do you even know this?"

"An old friend of mine told me."

"How does your old friend know?"

"He's Booker Lipton."

"*The* Booker Lipton?" Gale knew of Booker from her days covering Wall Street. "Rip, are you kidding me? Booker Lipton is a ruthless profiteer. He doesn't care about anything other than money, he's—"

Rip cut her off. "He's my friend." His eyes grabbed hers. "Do you know him?"

"No, but . . ."

"Don't believe everything you read."

"I don't, but I wrote some of it."

He laughed. "I'm sure Booker won't hold that against you." Rip went on to explain how Booker had always privately helped him, and recited a long list of the good Booker had also secretly done for others. Gale couldn't believe that Rip was describing a man, known as one of the most cut-throat tycoons since Rockefeller and the robber barons, as some sort of modern-day Robin Hood. "And that's just what *I* know about. I think half of the poor kids in the country are going to college on his dime."

"I had no idea."

"No one does. He prefers the shark image, which suits him well in business, but he wants the money for other reasons."

Gale knew for a fact that Booker had routinely destroyed whole communities by closing factories, shipping jobs overseas, and laying off tens of thousands. He had been investigated by nearly every US and European oversight agency in multiple industries, and twice been acquitted on bribery charges. But she saw no point in arguing anymore about him, as Rip seemed to only see Booker's alleged good side. She sliced a couple of apples into wedges. "I knew the Catholic Church had been involved in wars and tortures over the centuries, but that they're still resorting to such tactics in the modern era – it's hard to believe."

"It's true. Plots, murders, even worse . . . they've never stopped. The Vatican just developed its own stealth network and learned the value of good PR."

"So why did they kill Josh?" Gale cried. "Did they murder him in the name of God?"

"Sadly, there have been many others . . . so many others."

25

Larsen turned and stared at the pistol pointed at him. His options flashed – fight or flight – and neither seemed viable.

"Who are you?" he asked, holding up his hands.

"It's okay. I'm one of the good guys, so to speak," Janet Harmer said. "I work for Booker. We left you the note."

"You took out those agents?"

"Not for long. Four of them are just over the dunes looking for you."

"How do I know I can trust you?"

She looked at Larsen. "Man, I'm the *only* one you can trust right now. You're in way deep."

"If you're here to help me, why are you pointing a gun at me? Where's your green ball cap?"

Harmer looked down and smiled. She zipped the pistol in a hip pack. "You might have run, or pulled a weapon on me. Come on, let's get moving. We're out of time. The man in the green cap is waiting."

Larsen didn't want to make this choice. He wanted to be in Madagascar on a dig, anywhere but here. Instead, he licked his lips, thought of running, held back the frustrated, rage-filled scream welling inside, and simply asked, "Where are we going?"

"Let's keep on the way you're heading. We need to get to the car."

The beach grew more crowded every minute, especially down near the busy pier. The crowds worked well for Larsen and Harmer, who exited the dunes a few minutes later. They made it to the car moments before Lambert – the man in the green ball cap. Incredibly, the three of them were driving on 98-West heading to Panama City before the four agents realized that Larsen Fretwell had likely escaped the beach.

Hall nearly had to physically restrain Barbeau. He wanted to fly to Florida and "personally take the agents onto the pier and kick their asses." He simply could not believe the sloppiness.

"It's a flippin' repeat of Fredericksburg!" he shouted. "Why can't we get this right? Are we chasing Houdini here or what!?" He was fuming. They still didn't have a trace of Gaines, and now their two best leads – Sean Stadler and Larsen Fretwell – had slipped right through their fingers. To make matters worse, the FBI Director was on the phone for an update.

Earlier in his career, Barbeau had worked the Eric Rudolph case, the Olympic Park bomber who had eluded capture for five years by hiding out in the mountains of North Carolina. If this case went that way, Barbeau would be heading for a private sector job very soon. He and Hall were called back to Washington to regroup and reassess.

Hall phoned his girlfriend on the way. She was worried about the tension in his voice, his stress level, and asked if he'd been having bad dreams. "No," he lied, not wanting her to worry. Her concerns only added to his stress, and he knew she believed dreams were messages. If they were, and the past two nights were any indication of what was ahead, then finding Gaines might just become a real nightmare.

"Where are we going?" Larsen demanded as he continued to check the road behind them. Lambert was in the back seat, on the phone with Booker.

"Out of Florida as fast as we can," Harmer said, gripping the steering wheel with one hand while glancing at a map app on her phone with the other.

"Who were the guys at my house?"

"Lambert and I got there before sunrise and waited. The tough guy with the moustache showed up first. We're pretty sure he's a Vatican agent."

"A Vatican agent!?" Larsen was sure he'd heard wrong.

"Yeah. We're pretty sure," she said, lighting a cigarette.

"Even if the Vatican had thugs like that guy, which I don't believe, why would he be coming to see me?"

"He wasn't there for a weekend at the beach." Harmer took her eyes from the road long enough to give Larsen a "let this sink in" kind of look. "He was there to kill you."

"Why?"

She exhaled a thick stream of smoke. "Same reason they offed your buddy in Virginia."

"Josh? You're saying *Vatican* agents killed Josh?"

"Yes."

"Why?" Larsen demanded again.

"That, I couldn't tell you."

Larsen looked out the window while trying to grasp this insane story.

"Anyway," Harmer continued, "we surprised him and knocked him out cold, but he'll live. We'd just finished tying him up when the FBI showed. They sent only one agent into the house 'cause they figured it was empty. He was gonna wait while the other one took up a position on the beach. The other two agents got there after you."

"You assaulted a federal agent?" Larsen shook his head.

"As I said, he thought the place would be empty, so it was easy to get the drop on him. We stashed him in our makeshift holding cell, but couldn't stick around with more heat on the way. I wrote you the note, left it where you couldn't miss it, and we headed onto the beach."

"Is this a typical day for you? Beating up a priest and a cop?"

Harmer laughed loudly. "It ain't nothing but a thing."

"I'm going to get blamed for that – back there."

"He wasn't a priest, if that makes you feel better," Harmer said, still laughing.

"But the other one *was* an FBI agent? This is crazy."

"Don't worry," Lambert said from the back seat. "Booker Lipton is on your side. A little thing like the FBI shouldn't bother you." He patted Larsen's shoulder.

The Vatican agent was taken to a hospital with a concussion. Barbeau wanted him brought in for questioning, but an order came from above to release the man. An unhappy Dover threatened to cut off the ongoing updates his office had been providing, but he reconsidered based on promises from Rome that they would not interfere again.

Pisano redirected Nanski and Leary from Erie to check out Gale's place in Washington. Their next stop would be Harpers Ferry, a quaint, historic mountain town in West Virginia at the confluence of the Potomac and Shenandoah Rivers, where the constantly traveling Professor Ripley Gaines kept a small apartment. It was one of his favorite places, even if he spent less than four weeks a year there. The FBI had searched, and was watching both places. But, in spite of the assurances given to the Attorney General, Pisano needed more information.

26

Gale and Rip had decided to view the Eysen again back at the house, where he could take notes on his laptop. Topper was there, trimming the boxwood hedges when they returned.

Gale called out as Topper waved. "Care to join us for lemonade inside where it's cool?"

Rip pointed to his pack. "We need to do the Eysen."

"He's too old to be working out in this heat," Gale whispered. "I'm sure he won't stay long."

"Topper too old? He'll outlive us both. I promise you that."

Once inside, she poured them each a glass and asked Topper about the ruins.

Topper smiled. "Miss, you should know this old house keeps many secrets," he said in his thick southern drawl. He gestured toward the window. "The land has even more stories, but they get covered up with the fallin' leaves of time."

She took Topper's hand. "Tell me about those stories." Gale loved old people, and had a way of putting them at ease. She treasured their stories, and always asked a million questions.

Rip considered going outside alone to examine the Eysen.

"Oh, I haven't told those tales for a long time, Miss." He

smiled again and then looked out the window, past the trees, into another time.

"Topper, we don't want to bore Gale with a bunch of mountain history," Rip said.

"But she's in this here trouble with you, Ripley. Don't you think it's only right if she knows the beginnin' of it?" Topper asked, turning back to Rip.

Gale looked from Topper to Rip, stunned. "What's he mean, Rip? The beginning of what? How does he know about our trouble?"

"Topper, this isn't connected to that," Rip said, shaking his head.

"Connected to what?" Gale asked again. "How does he know?"

"Miss, some folks got troubles so great the trees talk about it years and years 'fore it comes."

"Topper, maybe you should head on home now," Rip said, standing up.

"No," Gale protested.

"Ripley, I've always known you to do the right thing . . . and rightly she *should* know."

"One of you better tell me what you're talking about."

"Damn it!" Rip exclaimed, pushing his hand through his shaggy brown hair. Ever since his mother's death when Rip was a teen, he'd had trouble trusting women. She'd promised repeatedly that the cancer wouldn't kill her. In the nearly twenty-five years since, his chiseled face, shy smile, and bright hazel eyes had left the often-brooding Rip with his pick of female companions. But thus far, none had been able to compete with ancient history. With Cosega found though, it might be time to trust someone else. He gave a single nod to Topper.

"'Cause you know, it begins this way. Ol' Mr. Scott always told us, you need to know these things. He said his granddad had put it to him that way. This line must carry on down, until it gets to where it needs to go," Topper said, looking at Rip. "It seemed a strange phrase at the time, but you know we always took that part to be important. Ol' Mr. Scott was a serious sort."

Topper lifted his glass, took a sip, then looked sadly into the bottom. Rip found the pitcher. "More lemonade?"

"Oh, good, yes, yes." He held a finger to his lips.

Gale patted his knee, "Topper, you were telling us . . ."

"It would be around 1937. I guess I was eight or nine then." He scratched his short grey hair and adjusted his gold-wire eyeglasses. "Ol' Mr. Scott was close to ninety then. See, my best friend was Billy Scott. He sold the place to Ripley's uncle, but old Mr. Scott was Billy's granddad."

"So he would have been born around 1846?" Gale asked.

"I remember he was born in 1847, on account of we had his hundredth birthday party a few weeks after I graduated high school, and that was in '47. That man lived to be a hundred and three." Topper laughed. "You know what? He learned to drive an automobile when he was seventy-two."

"And what did he tell you about this place Topper?"

"Yes, yes. You know he told us so many things. I reckon you'll be wantin' to know the mysteries. The secret room off the library is just the first, knowin' from the whispers."

Gale was confused. Rip silenced her with a glance.

"Back in the cabin days, before this place was built, in the time of ol' Mr. Scott's granddad, there were many folks comin' by on their way to someplace. See, then the stops with buildings were rare. You would just sleep in a field or in the woods. But when you could get to a cabin or so, then that was a busy place sometimes."

Gale nodded.

"So ol' Mr. Scott's granddad welcomed them in and he met all kinds of characters – mountain men, trappers, you know, holy people, Indians – Cherokee and Seminole – farmers, explorers, soldiers – the whole sordid lot on this young continent seemed to pass right by his old cabin."

In spite of her unsettledness, Gale was fascinated by this strange old man and his story. She refilled their glasses.

"That's tart. I like it that way." Topper smiled. "Anyhow, one day an old blacksmith came by and just, well, fell in love with the place. He was headin' somewhere or other, but he never did leave. And you know, back then once you have a blacksmith, you just about have a town." He walked over to one of the bookcases. "In no time at all, just a few years went by and people were settlin' in, maybe twenty families or so, and they decided to build a mighty church."

"My Clastier Castle," Rip said to Gale.

"Yes, son. That's a fact, and there was some story about why they wanted this kind of big place. I don't quite recall just now, but it was somethin' to do with one of them passersby. Yes, someone came by, stayed a while, and that was the reason they wanted such a big church." He took a long drink of lemonade, "But son, it's been too many years since I've thought about such things." Topper winked at Gale. "The shame of it was the church caught fire less than a year after it was done, when just about the whole town was inside."

"What happened?" Gale pleaded.

"See, the fire came in all around the church. The forest in flames and both doors were burnin'. They all huddled together in the back corner, kind of knowin' they were done for. Then the roof came down, and about that time, most of the survivors later said they saw a glowing star or somethin' up through the flames in the ceiling. Only it was daytime. Anyway, the roof fell toward the front of the building, the windows blew out, and most of the fire went with it. The woods still burned some ways yonder, but the fire was done and they all survived."

"Wow, how'd the fire go out?"

He looked at them both with a very serious expression. "On account of Clastier."

"Who was he?" she demanded.

"Oh, Miss, we were never to speak of him. It is the greatest of secrets."

"Still?" Gale begged.

"Sweet gal, it's even more a secret today than at the time of that terrible fire."

"What does Clastier have to do with the trouble we're in now? You said I should know."

Rip shook his head, but continued, reluctantly, to defer to Topper.

"Just two months ago, Frank Muller died in a motorcycle accident." Topper paused, his eyes focused on some distant place or time. "That leaves only two surviving descendants of the original builders." He closed his eyes for a long moment. "To my mind, there can't be much that the hunt for Clastier didn't affect. And," he said, opening his eyes, looking straight at Rip, "they're still searching."

"Who's searching? And who was Clastier?" Gale implored.

"It's a long way back to find the beginnings of his story. But you gotta start with the youngest descendant." He looked directly at Rip.

"You?" Gale asked Rip.

He nodded.

"You owe me these answers," Gale said. Rip had thought about telling her the whole story, and even wanted to show Topper the Eysen, but he'd been hoping to have more time to think about it. So much was at stake. Rip needed to know just what the Eysen contained. Here he was, with the man he trusted more than any other, and a woman he wasn't sure he should.

"There is danger in the knowing," Topper told Gale in an emotional tone. "You need to understand that a force you think is good in this world is something else, and they want Clastier silenced forever." He measured her face in order to gauge the impact. "The Vatican has been after Clastier for nearly two hundred years."

Gale looked at Rip in disbelief. "The Vatican?" she repeated.

"Clastier is long gone from us, but they know he left papers behind, and they have sought to destroy his words all this time."

"Is *that* why the Vatican is after us?" Gale asked Rip.

Topper raised an eyebrow.

"T-There's no connection," Rip stammered.

"Everything is connected," Topper corrected.

"They have no idea."

"Oh, Ripley. Come on now. They know *everything*. Rome ordered Clastier killed, they burned his church, and now they're after you. They want the remainin' descendants dead. Do you think Frank's motorcycle accident was really an accident?"

"If the Church had something to do with Frank's death, that's a separate case. But their pursuit of the Clastier Papers is unrelated to the Vatican's murder of Josh Stadler." Rip slapped the table. "They don't know I'm a descendant."

"And I thought you were supposed to be some kind of genius. Come on, boy."

"These supposed Christians kill anyone they perceive as a threat. They don't always stop to connect dots!" Rip shouted. "They don't know about a connection between Clastier and what I found because, other than my involvement in both, there *isn't* one."

Topper shook his head slowly. His face was etched by sun and secrets. "Some things get twisted from what they started as. I don't know what you found, but without Clastier you would not have discovered it."

"I can't deny that," Rip agreed, sighing.

"After two thousand years of consolidatin' power, it's impossible to add up the deaths and damage. The Church is more influential than any single nation, and you see, in the end power *always* corrupts," Topper said.

"Maybe in business and politics," Gale added, having a hard time with this new information, "but I know plenty of good, honest people who attend church every Sunday."

"Nothing wrong with that," Topper said. "I make an appearance at our local Unity Church every now and again myself." He winked. "But it's like most things. It isn't the citizens of a country that cause trouble in the world. It's their government. Wherever you find power, you'll find corruption. The Catholic Church is no different," Topper said, then turned his attention back to Rip. "If they don't know you're a descendant, then why are they after you?"

"Because of what I found."

Topper and Rip stared at each other for a long moment.

Finally, Topper put a shaky hand on Rip's shoulder. "Oh, my God. You *found* it?"

"Yes."

"And they know that?"

"Yes."

"Ripley, just how in the hell is it you're still alive?"

27

"Rip, you better tell me what's really going on here," Gale demanded.

"It's complicated."

"Then simplify it for me. What's in Clastier's papers?" Gale asked.

Rip looked at Topper.

"I'm assuming she knows what you found?" Topper asked.

Rip nodded.

"Then she should know why she'll likely be dead soon."

Gale's voice filled with anger. "You better talk fast Rip!"

"I hardly know where to begin."

She was about to explode when Topper placed his wrinkled hand on hers.

"Miss, maybe I can help. Let me take you back to the beginning. It's the only way to know where we are now."

She looked at him hesitantly.

"This story goes back to a time when not many European footprints had tracked this land. Ironically, Clastier himself was raised as a Catholic, maybe two hundred-fifty years ago in a tiny place up in the mountains of Northern New Mexico. A village of scattered settlements called Taos."

Rip, desperately wanting to get back to the Eysen, tried to excuse himself.

"Ripley, you might want to stay a minute and learn something new about something old," Topper said.

Rip let out an exasperated sigh.

"Mostly in those days," Topper continued, "indians still ruled the land, but Clastier's father was a French trapper. Not but a pocketful of French wanderin' those parts back then, and he didn't give the boy much more than his name. He left before his son even arrived. Clastier's mother was a Spanish woman, can't recall her name just now. Anyways, the boy grew up goin' to church, but also playin' mostly with Indian kids. They saw the mountains, canyons, and rivers as an endless playground." He chuckled, sipped his lemonade. "And I guess it was."

"Maybe the short version would be better Topper. Time is precious to us right now."

Gale shot Rip a disapproving look.

"Time is always precious." Topper smiled. "Okay, where was I? Clastier at that time would have been known by his first name, but it was lost to the ages and we know him only as Clastier. In fact, his youth is not much remembered except that he was exposed to the religious teachings of the Catholic Church and the spiritual ways of the Indians. His mother wanted him to become a priest, and he spent some years studying. He was very close with several important church leaders of the day, but somewhere in his twenties he started to split from the Church."

"Why?" Rip asked, knowing the answer, but wanting to keep Topper on the subject.

"Well, he had some kind of experiences, and began to see the church as limiting. Soon, he became vocal in his ideas and opposition. Then it didn't take long before people understood his points and he actually started to develop a following. Back then, Catholics were attemptin' to convert everyone on the planet, including the Native Americans.

"It doesn't seem to have stopped," Rip interrupted.

"That may be true, but in those days the Church wasn't as invincible. Back in Rome they saw Clastier as a threat to their missions in the New World. He was a real problem as his influence spread among the Indians and Spanish Catholics. Many of them abandoned the Church, and it could have easily led to the unraveling of organized religion in the New World."

"Jesus," Gale said.

"Well, not exactly, but the Bishop in Durango ordered the assassination of Clastier. He went into hiding at Taos Pueblo, where he wrote a summary of his beliefs and teachings. But soon church officials discovered his whereabouts and he fled into the mountains.

"Those were scary times, and Clastier's disappearance only increased his popularity. The story starts to get a little fuzzy from there, but at some point a devout follower escaped with the papers, and eventually brought them to relatives in Asheville. As he shared the story and writings with his family and neighbors, a group of them became so enraptured with Clastier that they decided to build a church to study the teachings of this great man. Membership grew until the fire occurred. No one ever did figure out how it started. Thing is, the rumors said that the papers survived, and for all these years there have been folks searchin' for them, includin' agents of the Holy See."

"Topper, do you know where they are?" Gale asked.

Topper winked. "I've read them, Miss," he said excitedly.

"I need to see them. Please," Gale said. The story was affecting her on a deeper level than she liked to admit.

"Miss, right from the first you reminded me of a dream that came several times some years back. A woman's voice asking, *'Where is Clastier?'* It must have been you."

Rip, still unsure, could see that Topper had made up his mind and nodded his agreement.

"Then it's decided." Topper patted her leg. "Maybe it's time they were finally published. How can the Church stop thousands of copies?"

"I don't know if it's time to publish," Rip said. He didn't believe the Vatican had yet connected him to the Clastier Papers, but it struck him that the same Church that had chased Clastier nearly two hundred years earlier to suppress something now pursued him for the same reason.

"I want to see them," Gale repeated.

"How 'bout you get me another glass of lemonade, and I'll get Clastier's papers."

Gale couldn't believe it. "You mean they're here? In this house?"

28

"When I used to read the papers as a teenager, I thought my uncle had brought them here from a safe deposit box or something. I had no idea they were kept here," Rip said.

"Been here all along," Topper said. "This place is even built with fire-stones from Clastier's church. Those papers are the reason the secret room was put in this house."

They followed Topper to the library. "We have the originals, and a translation done in the mid 1800s." He explained how many of the church survivors and their descendants met secretly in the house for almost a hundred and fifty years. However, over time, the first, and then next generation died off. Interest waned as the third generation scattered.

Rip had been sixteen when they first told him the whole story about Clastier. The mystical, religious, and spiritual parts of the story hadn't caught his imagination as it had some of the others. But the mysterious claims Clastier made and the story's historical aspects took root deep within him. His lineage to the church builders came through his mother. She had large sections of the papers memorized, but his father had always insisted she not discuss them with Rip. His uncle had secretly taught Clastier's legacy to Rip in an effort to move the information safely to the next generation. Now, the prior generation was gone, and only Rip and one cousin survived.

He shivered with the thought that if a bomb went off right then, Clastier would be lost forever. Some of the urgency had been lost through the years, but Clastier was more important now than ever.

Topper pointed to the east wall. "It's over there. Let's see how good you are at findin' things Professor."

The bookcases were part of the first construction – at least two hundred years old. The craftsmanship was fantastic – no nails, no visible gaps. Halfway down was the main support shelf, with wagons and children carved in pioneer scenes, wrapping the room. The books here were also old. The more modern titles occupied the wall near the entrance. Running his fingers along the smooth, dark wood, Rip almost couldn't believe Topper's story of a secret room. It would be the perfect place to hide the stone casing, which he'd already decided not to bring in the event they had to leave Asheville.

For ten minutes he searched before finding an almost invisible, half-inch peg at the back of the case. Gale helped him remove more books until he discovered that a similar peg was concealed in every other shelf about two feet from the corner. Once he had them all depressed, a nearly imperceptible click led him to the next step. He grabbed under the carving, where a child was doing a handstand on a stack of books, and all at once, a two-foot section of the shelf, nearly five-feet high, separated and swung into the library.

"Bravo." Topper smiled proudly. "It's all done with levers and weights."

"Ingenious. I never would have found it if I hadn't known it was here." Rip peered into the opening. Before him was a narrow room about four feet wide and six feet long. A very old oak desk that appeared to have been built in the room and a surprisingly comfortable-looking chair crowded the space. Books were stacked and filled three rows of shelves that ran along a low ceiling.

"Why wasn't I ever told about this room?" Rip asked.

"Your father forbade it. If you were seen anywhere near it, then he'd know you were studying Clastier," Topper whispered, as if Rip's father might hear.

Once inside the secret room, Topper removed the books from the top shelf and pushed several hidden pegs, causing a section of the ceiling to swing down and reveal a snugly concealed antique wooden box. He deftly pulled out Clastier's original papers; a stack of folded parchment, perhaps half an inch thick, between worn leather. The text was written in gorgeous script, every word in Old-World Spanish. Topper handed Gale a loosely bound book, again containing beautiful script though from a different hand than the previous papers. This one was in English. She moved her hand across the first page and read aloud.

English Translation
of
The Clastier Papers

We often wonder of the true value of Life. We search for endless years, as others have searched for endless ages.

I am a common man. I am not trying to teach you anything, for everything written here, or anywhere else, is already part of you. It seems obvious that each of us holds no greater responsibility than to assist one another. In the journey back to our souls, there are many, many obstacles. There are layers to cut through, thousands of years of civilization to let go of. Yet anything can be done in an instant – think of that. For as far as we

*seem to have drifted from the essential essence of ourselves, in truth, the
veil is very thin. Throughout our lives it is often lifted with a breeze, but
we seldom pay attention.*

*Therefore, I am merely telling you what I have seen and remem-
bered. If it helps you to remember, then you will remind me and show me.
We must do this because none of us will completely return to their soul
until we all return. This is why the more you help others, the more you
are helped – it has always been this way.*

*There is something else we all must know . . . there is deception
within the Church that drives confusion and fear. Nothing should preach
separation, for we are all one.*

*There is a day in the past, and another in the future, which mirror
each other, and the same events repeat. The past can change the future,
and the future changes the past.*

Rip recalled the first time he had read the papers after his mother's death. He'd become obsessed with Clastier's writings. It had
been nearly two decades since he'd last held the papers he'd all
but memorized.

They were divided into two sections: *The Attestations,* and *The
Divinations.* The former was the bulk of the work, and
comprised his teachings and philosophies. But The Divinations –
a series of predictions for the future, most of which had already
come to pass – was the part that had captured young Rip's imagination and sent him into the world seeking something that likely
didn't exist. He had found it intoxicating to be one of only a few
people in the world to hold and know such secrets; information
so provocative that Popes had sought its complete destruction.
Topper and his uncle had told him Clastier's story and let him
read the translation, but only a few were trusted to know where
the original documents were hidden.

But that didn't matter because Clastier's words, the way he
alluded to ideas, explained mysteries with more mystery, took

root in Rip and wouldn't let go. He'd seen the papers as a complex treasure map, and had chosen archaeology in order to find what Clastier promised lay hidden. One of The Divinations, specifically, ignited the passion that propelled him to find the thing from the past that would change the future.

And now that he had, it threatened everything.

29

Harmer, Lambert, and Larsen drove straight to the bus station in Panama City, Florida. The sleepy attendant seemed surprised as they all rushed through the doors. Another Booker employee, just leaving the counter, met them.

"Not enough options here, but we could get him on a bus to Jacksonville and onto a train from there," the man said.

"The feds are probably only minutes behind us," Lambert said.

"Highway, train, plane, boat, that's a lot for the FBI to cover," Harmer said.

"Jesus, you guys don't have a plan!?" Larsen blasted.

"We do. In fact, we have several," Lambert replied.

"Then pick one!"

"Remember, the best plans are the ones that can change as circumstances do," Harmer added, eyeing a no smoking sign suspiciously.

Larsen shook his head. A rapid discussion ensued.

Lambert got Delta Airlines on his cell phone and booked a flight to Atlanta leaving in twenty minutes. From there, they could go anywhere.

"Booker has a remote home in Montana. He wants us to get

you there until he can figure this all out," Harmer told Larsen as they left the bus station. "Don't worry, we've got a good plan."

"I thought you had several," Larsen said.

"We've got several good plans," Harmer corrected. "We'll split up at the airport, making it harder for them to find us."

Lambert found a short-term parking space and they raced to the terminal. There were two of them, no bags to check, not even any carry-on. The ticket agent remembered when the FBI questioned her an hour and twenty minutes later. She only glanced at their IDs, but recalled clearly that Larsen Fretwell had been one of the men who boarded the flight to Atlanta.

"He was very tall," she said.

The flight took sixty-four minutes. They were moving through the busiest passenger airport in the world as the first agents arrived. Lambert noticed the feds scanning the crowd, but somehow they made it to the airport shuttle undetected. The bus dropped them off at the Grand Escape, a stunning six-story hotel, part of a worldwide chain of some 2,800 owned by Booker. Calls had been made, an emergency exit left propped open, and surveillance cameras stalled or reset. They picked up keys at the front desk to a room they never intended to use, then took the elevator to the top floor suite.

The plan called for a helicopter to pick them up on the roof in fifteen minutes. It would be tricky because the only part of the roof open and flat enough for a landing was on the other side of the dramatic pyramid atrium. A narrow catwalk, in place for wiring and accessible only from a panel in the supply closet next to the entrance to the stairs, was their best escape route.

They were halfway across the catwalk when the FBI entered their room and began filtering onto all the other floors. At the same time, agents spotted them from below. A burst of commands across walkie-talkies and bullhorns followed. Before the fugitives could reach the other side, the SWAT team lowered men onto the roof. Officers rushed onto the catwalk from both ends.

"Don't worry," Lambert said. "There'll be a lawyer waiting for us when we reach the federal building." As he raised his hands in surrender, he heard an awful wrenching sound of twisting metal. The expression of terror on the face of the closest FBI agent was the last thing he saw. The entire two-hundred-foot platform collapsed.

The report devastated Barbeau when he received word twenty minutes later that Larsen, his accomplice, five federal agents, and four SWAT officers had plummeted to their deaths.

Nine law enforcement dead. The media would be in a frenzy, and another key lead was gone.

After ten minutes of reading, Gale didn't want to stop, not even to watch the Eysen. She felt as if the Clastier Papers had been written just for her. Rip took Topper outside and set the Eysen on the patio table.

"I can't believe what I'm seeing," Topper said after they got to the part of the spinning Earth. "How could this be that old?"

"It's impossible," Rip said.

Topper slowly took his eyes off the Eysen and looked deeply into Rip's. "Impossible . . . like it says in the Divinations? I never thought I'd see it."

Topper and Rip knew Clastier's writings well. Rip recalled the lines from one Divination that had been burned into Rip's mind since he had first read the pages as a teen.

"There will be a time at the beginning of the twenty-first century whence the earth shall reveal an impossible object. Within the stone is a light which will cause the holy city to collapse, for it shall erase the past, demonstrate all knowledge to be false, and the scriptures to be a hoax."

Most of Clastier's predictions had already come to pass, or Rip may not have been so consumed by that one. Clastier had accurately foretold the rise of the United States, Hitler's atrocities during World War II, the development and dropping of the atomic bomb, the moon landing, and many other events. There were only five remaining Divinations left after *the impossible object*, and each carried its own view of an extraordinary future.

But now one of Clastier's forecasts – the Eysen – had come to life in front of his eyes. "It's true."

"And this means the five final Divinations are assured," Topper said with reverence.

The Eysen, without being touched, cycled through its sequence and went beyond any point Rip had previously witnessed. Suddenly, an image appeared that made Rip gasp.

30

The human image looking at them from within the Eysen appeared so lifelike that, for a moment, Rip thought the person might speak to them. Instead, the man stared stoically while tears streamed down his face. Topper turned to Rip with a questioning look, but Rip couldn't take his eyes off the man. Finally, Rip whispered to Topper, "Get Gale."

The man in the Eysen appeared to nod ever so slightly.

"Can he see us?" Topper asked, barely audible.

"*Get Gale*," Rip repeated.

Gale heard an abrasive sound as if being awakened from a dream, and almost resented the intrusion. Deep into The Attestations and yet to discover The Divinations, Gale reluctantly answered Topper.

"Miss, come quickly. Ripley wants you to see something in the Eysen!"

Gale complied, rushing outside with Topper.

The Crying Man was more than a fair trade for interrupting Gale's first reading of the Clastier Papers, still clutched in her hands. None of them could have explained it to anyone who wasn't there, who hadn't felt it. The Crying Man somehow communicated with each of them separately and profoundly. He stared into their eyes. His ancient tears carried wisdom and messages seemingly meant just for them.

"It's like something psychic," Gale said, reaching to touch the glass, wanting to be sure it was really there, separating her from this sacred man. "He can see us!" Her tone was hushed and urgent.

"Can you?" Rip asked, not believing his own question.

The man's gaze expressed emotions impossible to conjure in so short a time. They wouldn't know until later, but Gale, Rip, and Topper had each seen different things, understood different truths, and each would have sworn the apparition inside the Eysen had spoken individually in an unknown, yet universal language.

The screen suddenly went blank. Topper nodded and turned away, then quietly, sadly, walked away.

Gale and Rip didn't move, hardly breathed as they tried to memorize everything the Crying Man had conveyed. Although they would never forget the Crying Man, those first moments after he vanished were what it must have felt like to be suspended in time, immersed in complete understanding. They struggled to assimilate it with the mundane lives they had lived up to that point. Clinging to what they saw like a fading dream, they were both forever changed.

"We've lived before," Gale murmured.

"And we've lost far greater societies than exist now. Than we ever knew existed," Rip said.

"How much power does the human mind possess? If it can survive millions of years, and communicate so much . . . Do you realize what we're capable of?"

"Everything."

Knowing whether the Crying Man had actually communicated individually with them was something they were unable to agree on, because later when they discussed it their collective knowledge of the viewing merged, and there was no way to know who had experienced what.

Gale and Rip turned in early so they could resume studying the Eysen at sunrise. The Eysen had not come back on since the Crying Man, but they knew it would, and they'd see him again.

Gale drifted off while reading the Clastier Papers, but Rip could not find sleep. He suddenly remembered the awards banquet he should have been attending that night in Miami. It was the first time since the discovery of the Eysen that he had thought about the Archaeologist of the Year Award and its $50,000 grant money. He considered how, just a week earlier, he'd reached the pinnacle of his career.

Now he was a fugitive, wanted by the FBI and targeted by the Vatican.

31

Nanski spotted the Bureau car forty feet from Gale's front door. Parking was at a premium in this part of D.C. "The feds probably towed some poor guy's car just so they could scope out her house," Nanski told Leary.

"Yeah, and it's a waste of time. She's not going to come near this place." Nanski grumbled at the sight of another agent watching the building's rear entrance. "I guess they're going to make us do this the hard way."

They parked at the end of the block in a barely legal space and quickly crossed to the fire escape of the end unit. They were on the backside of the row houses, invisible to the feds, who could see only the alley entrances. Leary climbed up, and then pulled Nanski onto the roof. The two men kept low as they crawled carefully along the steep metal roof until they were directly across from the back of Gale's house. The feds' view was blocked by the building that they were on, so Nanski and Leary just had to climb down one fire escape, and then go back up the one leading to Gale's.

The lock picked easily. Bypassing the alarm proved a bit trickier, but it was not a sophisticated system. With four federal agents watching, they couldn't do a thing until morning when they could work unnoticed in daylight.

"Ever see what a wintergreen lifesaver does in the dark?" Leary asked, snapping a candy between his teeth.

Nanski watched the resulting tiny fluorescent sparks for a few seconds. "Let's get some sleep."

After praying, each found a couch. They knew that if they got caught it would be an embarrassment for the Church, but ultimately, Dover would protect their operation. They slept soundly.

Saturday July 15th

Nanski and Leary were already moving when the first sunlight filtered in. They opened and inspected every drawer and cabinet. The FBI report had indicated that she traveled with her laptop and didn't have a desktop computer, but their job included looking for more casual information; something that would reveal why she had run and where she had gone.

As always, they were thorough, but very neat. Everything was photographed. Only a book was taken, which Nanski had noticed while scanning Gale's shelves. Through the profile he knew Gale opposed organized religion. Why then did she possess a copy of *De Ente Et Essentia* (Thomas Aquinas' *On Being and Essence*)? It seemed odd, until he read the inscription and saw who had given her the book. Then it seemed incredible.

Leaving was much easier than entering. They simply exited the back door, walked down the alley, and emerged within fifteen feet of one of the stakeout vehicles. The FBI would have had no way of knowing which house they had left because they couldn't see into the alley. The two Vatican agents uploaded the digital images and reported the information about the book to Pisano. Within an hour, they would be carefully ransacking Rip's place in

Harpers Ferry with the same questions: Why did he run? Where did he go?

FBI Special Agent Dixon Barbeau joined Attorney General Harrison Dover at the press conference. Noticeably absent was the FBI Director. A cover story was put forward about an ongoing investigation. No names could be released pending notification of next of kin. The alleged crimes were only hinted at – domestic conspiracy that included theft of government property and plots to cause unrest and disorder. They rebuffed a reporter's question about terrorism, but did not deny it.

The point of their joint appearance was essentially to provide filler for the networks, which had to say something about nine dead cops. But the feds didn't want the story to grow, and had decided to stonewall. Instead, toward the end, they produced the name and photo of a second-rate criminal who had been indicted, but not arrested, for arms dealing and other related charges. He actually had nothing to do with the case, but the Attorney General declared him a person of interest.

A national manhunt commenced. The media had its distraction.

Back in the halls and away from the press, the Attorney General delivered a stern lecture to Barbeau. Next, Dover provided a backstory for each victim of the catwalk collapse at the Grand Escape Hotel. Finally, he revealed new details about the incident that stunned Barbeau.

"With all due respect, Mr. Attorney General, I think that proves we're dealing with more than an impulsive archaeologist and a nature writer here."

"Of course we are, Barbeau. But tell me, who is helping them and why? This is the most important case of your career. If you embarrass me again, it will be your last."

"Mr. Attorney General, if this, as you say, is the most important case of my career, I must be missing something. If you've read my file, you'd know—"

"Don't insult my intelligence Special Agent Barbeau. This is your most important case because I say it is. Do you need to be reminded that your boss reports to me?"

"No sir."

"Then stop wasting time and go do your job while you still have it!"

32

Having told his parents all he knew about Josh's death, Sean managed to talk them out of going to the police or the media until they knew more. They were reluctant, but because of the official cause of death and virtually no evidence at the scene, it seemed unlikely anyone would believe Sean's story. However, they would insist on an autopsy.

His father made an appointment with a top criminal defense attorney for Monday, the earliest available time. Sean took a shower and put on fresh clothes, then found his parents in the living room.

"Yesterday I woke up and my life was perfect," his mother said weakly. "Now one son is dead, and the other is wanted by the FBI. How did this happen?" She couldn't stop the tears.

His father put an arm around her. "Listen to me Sean. You need to stay somewhere else. The FBI may be here any time to arrest you. How about with your old high school friend John until we can meet with the attorney?"

"Okay. But can they really arrest me?"

"Sean, you may think you were just doing a favor for Josh by giving a ride to two friends of his, but when I talked to the attorney about making an appointment, he told me that if in fact those two were knowingly fleeing federal prosecution, you can be charged with a number of crimes, including aiding and abetting. And what if Gale Asher and Ripley Gaines had something to do with Josh's murder?"

"No way," Sean said.

"How do you know? You just met them," his father said as his mother sobbed again.

"Josh told me he'd known Gale for years. Gaines is an archaeologist, not a murderer. They're running scared."

"Why are they running? Why are they afraid of the FBI?"

"Come on, Dad. How many times was Josh arrested for demonstrating against war? The government isn't always right."

"I know that, but something is going on that we don't know anything about."

"I know one of my sons is dead," his mother began. "And I don't want to lose my other one!"

A knock at the front door sounded like a gunshot to their frayed nerves. Sean and his parents exchanged terrified looks. Sean ran for the back door. He wove between dunes and houses, making it four blocks down the beach before his father opened the front door.

During his breathless run he didn't think of being caught. Instead, his brother filled every thought. Wanting Josh's death to count for something, needing answers, and devastated by the tragic expressions of his parents, Sean decided to return to Asheville.

His plan grew more out of desperation than logic. He boarded a bus from Virginia Beach to Asheville with a $121 ticket. The twenty-two-hour trip would give him plenty of thinking time. Something he needed, but didn't want.

Sean's mistake was paying with a credit card. In less than twenty minutes the FBI knew his destination. Half an hour later, agents were following the bus. Barbeau gave orders not to arrest him until he led them to Gaines and Asher.

"But, by God," he said, "don't let this punk get away!"

"Sean Stadler might not be heading to Gaines," Hall cautioned. "Our research shows no evidence that the three knew each other before six days ago."

"He's going somewhere, and he's our only real lead at the moment," Barbeau said, opening a pack of M&M's.

Hall nodded. "The twenty agents we just deployed to Asheville will be there long before that bus arrives. Virginia and North Carolina State Police have been alerted. No one is getting off that bus without our seeing it.

"Get two agents on that bus. Make sure they're competent, young, and that they don't look like us."

Rip's place in Harpers Ferry presented a problem to the Vatican agents. His loft apartment, located above a fancy gift shop, had only one entrance; a narrow staircase accessed from Washington Street. The balcony on the back, with its view of the river, could not be reached from the ground. It might have been possible to get in from the roof, but the feds had the front and the back well covered.

"Jesus loves me, yes, I know, 'cause the Bible tells me so. Jesus loves me . . . " Leary sang softly.

"Why are they wasting this manpower?" Nanski asked. "These two are too smart to return to their homes."

"We need a diversion," Leary suggested before resuming his song.

"A diversion big enough to pull an FBI agent off-post would require approval from Pisano," Nanski said, dialing. "He's not picking up."

They decided to wait and hope they got lucky, at least until they could reach Pisano. Leary blended in with the tourists and watched the agent watching the front, while Nanski sat in the car and took the one in back.

Nanski couldn't help but think about the amount of

resources the government had put on a case that normally wouldn't require more than a few forest rangers, and maybe a couple of state cops. He knew the Church was applying as much pressure as possible without wanting to show how much was at stake.

He said a prayer of thanks that a good Catholic like Harrison Dover was the U.S. Attorney General. After an hour, Nanski tried Pisano again.

"The feds have just moved on Asheville, North Carolina. We're sending a helicopter for you. You'll be in Asheville in less than three hours." Pisano told him where to be for the pickup.

"What about Gaines's apartment?"

"Forget it. We've just been granted access to the stuff the feds took out of there on Wednesday. If we don't catch them today, we'll get someone else to hit his place."

Nanski drove around the block and pulled up to Leary.

"Change of plans," Nanski said.

"Again?"

"Strange case, this one. But Lord willing, this will be the final day for Mr. Gaines and Ms. Asher."

33

Gale and Rip had been frustrated for most of the morning. The Eysen acted entirely differently from the way it had on their previous viewings. The sequence began with lights, but only for a few seconds before blinking off to black, and then incredibly to random flashes of faces. Rip tried moving his hands, pressing the surface, spinning it to other positions, but nothing worked. Gale continued reading Clastier, enraptured by the spiritual depth of the man who had written the secret text.

"It's like he knew everything," she said. "Where did he get all these answers, and how did he know so much about the future?"

They were just breaking for lunch when a car sped down the long driveway in a cloud of dust. Rip grabbed the Eysen and stuffed it in his pack at the same time Gale shoved the English translation of the Clastier Papers in hers. They darted to the far side of the house and made for the trees. Only when they were safely concealed did they chance a look back.

"It's Topper," Rip said, trying to catch his breath.

"Why did he drive? And is he always such a speed demon?"

"No. Just to be safe, let's watch for a minute."

"He's alone," Gale said as they saw Topper come out of the house.

"So it seems."

"Ripley, there's trouble," Topper shouted from the backyard. He shifted directions, cupped his hands around his mouth, and yelled again. "Ripley, Gale, are you there?"

Rip stepped out. "Over here."

"Come quick!" Topper hollered, waving his arm.

"Wait here," Rip said to Gale as he handed her his pack.

"Ripley, you've got to go," Topper said, as soon as Rip reached him. "The FBI knows you're here."

"How?" Rip looked over his shoulder at the driveway and then to Gale.

"You remember the Hamilton boy?"

"No."

"It doesn't matter. I just ran into him at the farm supply. He's a state trooper, and they just called him in on his day off. A big operation. The feds are pourin' into town."

"Damn it."

"Take my car."

"Maybe it's not us."

"That's not all. The radio is filled with reports of nine law enforcement officers being killed while trying to arrest a fugitive wanted for theft of government property."

"That couldn't have anything to do with us. No cops have died."

"The wanted man also perished. An archaeologist named Larsen Fretwell."

Rip covered his eyes with one hand and sank to the ground. Gale ran over.

"Sorry, son." Topper gripped Rip's shoulder. He repeated the news to Gale. "You have to go."

"This is totally out of control," Gale said, crying.

They packed up in minutes. Rip reluctantly left the casing locked in the secret room with the original Clastier Papers. Gale carried the English translation in her pack. Rip had the Odeon and the Eysen in his. They'd photographed the casing from every angle with Topper's digital camera, and Rip could continue to study the photos on his laptop from the road.

"I packed you some food in the car," Topper said. "You might not want to stop. I'll stay here and keep an eye on things."

"Hopefully the FBI won't find the connection to my relatives here."

"The bigger worry is if the Vatican agents figure out you're a descendant."

"That's an awfully big leap for them to make," Rip said, staring out the car window at his old friend for a moment. Topper had helped raise him. Clastier wasn't the only secret they shared.

The silence of their farewell was shattered by the loud roar of an approaching helicopter. Rip scooped up his pack and grabbed the door handle, ready to run. Gale cradled hers, guarding the Clastier Papers. Topper looked up. The trees partially shielded them, but their car was visible from the air.

"They can't know we're in the car," Rip reminded Gale.

"Depends on who's in that bird," Topper said. It made several more passes before giving up. They watched the chopper fly off, devastated that the feds really were in Asheville, and wondered if it was already too late to slip out of town.

Twenty minutes away from the house, Gale suddenly pulled over into an elementary school parking lot and began sobbing uncontrollably.

"Gale, what's wrong?" Rip asked.

"Larsen is dead. It's too much," she said between soft sobs.

Rip was surprised by her intense reaction. Larsen had been his closest friend and somehow he was holding together. "Gale, come on. You weren't this upset when Josh died. You hardly knew Larsen."

"That's not true. We were together. We'd been dating for a couple of months."

At first Rip was speechless. "That's why you were there?" he said quietly.

She nodded and wiped her eyes.

"Why didn't you tell me?"

"Larsen didn't want to. He knew how mad you were and figured it would make you angrier."

"It does." He didn't want it to, but he couldn't shake it.

"I'm sorry."

"Me, too." Rip studied her. "How serious were you?"

"He'd been working so much, but it was getting there. We met when I covered his dig in Alberta last year, but it wasn't until he ran into Josh a few months back and my name came up that things really began. Josh gave him my number. I was at the camp that day to tell him we either had to get serious or part ways."

"What did he say?"

"We never got the chance to have that talk. You showed up and we found the Eysen instead. I've lost two dear friends in two days."

Rip hugged her. "We have to go."

When Booker heard the news about all the deaths in the Atlanta Grand Escape Hotel disaster, he immediately phoned Kruse, who was just leaving his Knoxville office to drive the two hours to Asheville.

A loner, Kruse had been with AX, Booker's security service, ever since a long-retired senior officer had recruited him out of college. During the intervening ten years, Kruse had become one of the go-to guys in AX. Raised in a military family, he cherished honor and loyalty above all else. A good fit for Booker.

Kruse had the look of a commando, although he'd never

served in the armed forces, a fact that bothered him. Still, he'd
traveled the world for Booker, and had seen a fair amount of
action. Three ghosts visited from time to time, but Kruse didn't
put up with tormenting memories of people he'd killed. They'd
all deserved it. Protecting people and getting them out of
trouble sometimes got messy. They once asked him to serve in
Black-AX, an elite crew within AX populated by former special
ops soldiers who routinely did assassinations and other nasty
deeds, but he had declined. Although Kruse could handle
trouble when it came, he didn't like to go looking for it.

He was intrigued by what he'd been able to piece together
about Gaines from the news and the briefs he received from AX.
He looked forward to meeting the man who had become a reck-
less obsession for his normally careful employer. Kruse didn't
know that this would turn out to be his most dangerous
assignment.

"It's nothing less than divine intervention," Pisano told Nanski.
"When we heard that Sean Stadler had boarded a bus to Asheville, North Carolina, we routinely cross-checked all the data we
had about this case in our computers."

"Same as the FBI," Nanski said.

"Yes, but we have access to their computers, too, and that is
not a luxury they enjoy. No one has access to the Vatican's data-
base. Our computers contain an obscure fact about Mr. Gaines.
It seems his cousin is the beneficiary of a small trust fund. One
of the assets of that trust is a secluded home outside of
Asheville."

"How convenient," Nanski said.

"Far beyond convenient. This is a house the Church has tried
to purchase on numerous occasions. In fact, our agents have
covertly entered the home three times during the past century."

"Divine intervention sounds like the only explanation,"

Nanski said, smiling, although the news caused him some uneasiness. "We are meant to find Gaines and Asher. To recover the artifacts before the FBI does."

"Yes," agreed Pisano. "I've emailed you the floor plans to the house, the layout of the grounds, and the locations of neighboring homes."

Nanski wanted to ask Pisano why the Church had tried to buy the property, and was even more curious as to why they had broken in three times over the course of a hundred years, but he would save those questions for the Cardinal in Rome. He tried to concentrate on the matter at hand, but he had a terrible feeling that rather than being close to resolution, the crisis was widening.

The fact that the two biggest, seemingly unrelated threats to the Church in the modern era had a common denominator – a brilliant archaeologist named Ripley Gaines – terrified him. The fact that accompanying Gaines was a former investigative reporter, a liberal-minded woman, no less who owned a copy of *De Ente Et Essentia* was with Gaines, shook his very being.

34

Dixon Barbeau waited in the reception area outside the Director's office in the J. Edgar Hoover Building. He'd never met the current Director. The prior Director had brought him in twice during the Rudolph investigation, and those hadn't been pleasant experiences. Tired and frustrated, he expected this to be less of a meeting and more of a chewing out, a continuation of the Attorney General's lecture. Instead, when he entered the private office, the Director came around his desk and shook Barbeau's hand.

"You look awful, Dixon."

"It's been a rough week."

"That's an understatement, huh? Each day getting worse." The Director sat on the edge of his desk and stared at Barbeau. "Grand Escape Hotel, Atlanta . . . one of the worst days in the Bureau's history. I couldn't make the press conference because the President had summoned me to the White House."

Barbeau looked surprised. He had wondered, as had many reporters, why the Director of the FBI hadn't appeared on such a dark day. "I'm sorry."

"I know you are. But I'm not blaming just you. There's plenty of blame to go around. The engineers who designed that damn catwalk for one, the hotel owner, the local law enforcement, me, you . . . it's a long list. Mostly though, it was just damn bad luck." He walked to his window and glanced down at the city. "The President asked for my resignation."

Barbeau couldn't hide his surprise. The Director stared back, assessing him.

"Are you asking me to resign?" Barbeau stood.

"No, Dixon. You're not a big enough scapegoat. The President has reconsidered my position, but this is a tricky business you and I have landed in." He watched Barbeau closely.

"I'm not sure I follow you, sir."

"The President didn't want my resignation because of those tragic deaths in Atlanta."

Barbeau remained baffled. "Then why?"

"He wanted my resignation because Ripley Gaines has not been apprehended. Capturing Gaines and recovering the artifacts, in the President's words, 'is the highest priority for the Bureau, and a grave matter of concern for our national security.' Now, please tell me why that is."

The two men stood eye-to-eye.

"Sir, I cannot even begin to imagine what part of this case would cause the President of the United States to make such a statement."

"You're missing something Dixon. Think about everything you know concerning this situation. Gaines, Asher, the artifacts, the dead photographer, Larsen Fretwell . . . what?"

Barbeau sat down and remained silent for several minutes. The Director returned to the window and stared out across the cityscape of the Nation's capital.

"What the hell are these artifacts?" Barbeau finally asked.

"That's all I can think of too."

"You mean you don't know?" Barbeau had thought he was being tested.

"No. I pressed the President, but he declined to provide further details, saying that the investigation was my department.

When I told him more information would help me bring this to a quicker resolution, he said, 'not necessarily.' It's puzzling, to say the least."

"What made him change his mind, if I may ask?"

"Five minutes after I arrived, the President took a phone call. Afterwards, he said I could have a little more time to resolve the matter. That's when he launched into the part about how critical it was to capture Gaines, but refused to say more. He abruptly ended the meeting, and an aide ushered me out."

"I assume you've spoken to the Attorney General."

"He is on the same page with the President. In fact, they are meeting again as we speak."

"Director, may I be blunt?"

"Please."

"Why didn't he fire you? What changed his mind?"

"He may be saving me as a scapegoat. Based on what he said, the Atlanta nightmare is minor compared to the stakes of this investigation. If something goes wrong, there are ultimately three highly visible people to blame . . ."

"The President, the Attorney General, and the Director of the FBI," Barbeau finished his statement.

"Exactly," the Director said.

"So back to the original question . . . the artifacts."

"Let me tell you what we've learned in the past twenty-four hours."

Kruse approached the Asheville house cautiously. The old car in the driveway definitely didn't look like a rental. He hadn't expected trouble, and now wished another AX agent had accompanied him. After pulling out his Glock-19 handgun, he circled the large house cautiously, looking in windows where possible. The humidity hung in the absence of a breeze, and he missed his car's air conditioning. Chirping birds broke the eerie silence.

The door off the back deck was open. The screen door wasn't even latched, and squeaked when he opened it. He stood there absorbing the sounds of the house. Too quiet. Gaines and Asher could be asleep, but fugitives napping at that hour of the day with the back door open seemed unlikely.

Even though he sensed that the house was empty, experience had taught him to be alert. Room by room he searched, thoroughly. *Big. Damn. House,* he thought. Time to hit the second floor.

Even before he stepped onto the wide staircase, he saw the body.

35

Rip pushed himself onto the floor of the rental car's back seat, figuring he was the more wanted of the two. Gale pulled her blonde curls into a ponytail and stuffed it under a ball cap. She drove past what she believed were plainclothes agents in a sedan. A state trooper slowed as he passed in the opposite direction, but no one stopped her. After crossing the French Broad River, she told Rip he could sit up. Traffic grew heavier.

"Too many cars for a Sunday. The FBI must have a roadblock set up on I-40 that's slowing everything down," Rip said.

"Check the map. Find us another route," Gale said.

"Here, follow signs to Smokey Park Highway. That turns into US-19 and runs parallel to 40. If we can make it to Jonathan Creek Road, we'll be able to pick up the interstate again well past the roadblock."

"Get down!" Gale yelled. Two state troopers were driving toward them. As soon as they passed, she sighed with relief. A helicopter flew low, but it turned out to be a news-chopper covering interstate traffic. She turned on the radio and found a local talk station. They had interrupted their Saturday oldies program for updates on the breaking story.

The announcer described backups on interstates leaving

Asheville in four directions. So far the North Carolina State Police had declined to comment on the subject of their search. Law enforcement helicopters were also doing aerial sweeps of the area. Officials were working to close Hendersonville Road, Smokey Park Highway, Merrimon Avenue, and the Blue Ridge Parkway.

"I'm looking for alternate routes," Rip said. "There are a bunch of secondary roads. They'll never be able to cover them all."

"This is nuts. Where are they getting all this manpower?"

"And why?" Rip asked. "Someone knows exactly what we have."

"Yeah, someone who knows a lot more about it than we do," Gale said. "Oh, my God. Look!"

She pointed to the incoming lanes of the interstate they had just passed under. The sight terrified her more than anything that had happened so far. A convoy of military vehicles exited onto the ramp.

"There must be fifty of them!"

Just then the radio announcer stopped his ramblings and said, "Word just in from News Ten's copter crew that a substantial number of National Guard troops have entered Asheville from the west. We'll try to confirm if this is an actual deployment, and if this is connected to the roadblocks."

"We've got about twenty miles or so until Jonathan Creek Road. Hopefully getting back on I-40 won't be a mistake."

"Then where?" Gale asked.

"Booker is our only hope."

Another chopper flew overhead. Not far behind, they could see another roadblock being set up.

"We might make it," Gale said. "Are you sure we can trust Booker?"

"I'm sure," Rip said.

"Maybe we should find someone we know we can trust, someone who can help us make sense of the Eysen."

"I'm all for that. Any suggestions?"

"Clastier."

"He's been dead for more than a hundred years."

"That doesn't mean he can't help us."

"Where do you suggest we find him?

"Taos, New Mexico."

"You want to go two thousand miles to the high desert of northern New Mexico to find some dead man? How is that going to help us? Why don't we just let Booker stash us somewhere really safe?"

"They found Asheville, so don't you think they'll find Booker? This is the FBI, the Vatican, and God knows who else. They can find your connection to Booker."

"Maybe, but Booker's pretty powerful himself."

"So is Clastier, and there's no way they can connect us to him."

"I think you're losing it Gale."

"Taos is as good a place as any to hide."

"Have you ever even been there?"

"No."

"So maybe it's *not* a very good place to hide. Not to mention we're short on cash and would need to sneak across the whole damn country to get there."

"Rip, I know it sounds weird, but I think Clastier will protect us."

"How could he?"

"You've spent your life looking for something in his Divinations."

"Clastier's a proven prophet. He was an amazing man, but—"

"This is meant to be. Do you think we just happened to wind up together?"

"Gale, you followed me."

"But why was I there? We didn't find the Eysen by accident, and you didn't simply happen to grow up reading Clastier. There's just no such thing as a coincidence."

36

Kruse, Booker's employee, climbed the grand staircase slowly. With his Glock cocked and ready, he stopped after each step to listen. By the time he reached the body at the top, he believed he was alone in the southern mansion.

The wiry old man had no pulse. Nothing. Kruse carefully fished a wallet out of the dead man's pocket. Topper Windom. He lived next door. No sign of foul play. Poor guy probably took the stairs too fast and had a heart attack. Wonder what he was doing in the house? Probably hasn't been dead too long.

After quickly searching the rest of the place, Kruse called Booker.

"Check the body again, very carefully. If he's in that house where Rip's been for two days, then his death is suspect. Remember, the medical examiner falsely ruled the photographer Stadler's death as heart failure," Booker said. "Someone may have beat you there."

After taking a couple of minutes to study the body more closely, Kruse picked up his phone. "I'm no medical examiner, but I don't see anything unusual. The guy was old. He's at the top of a staircase. It seems pretty logical, at least under normal circumstances. Want me to try to get a blood sample?"

"Nothing normal about any of this. Forget the blood. No doubt you'll have company any minute. Is there *any* sign of Rip or the woman? Any clue as to where they went?"

"Nothing. Maybe the feds got them."

"I've got a pretty good source. If they'd been arrested, I'd know."

"Asheville is like an ant hill filled with cops and feds," Kruse said. "The Vatican guys can't be far behind."

"I think the Vatican guys beat the FBI again."

"You think they killed this old man?"

"Yes."

"Why?"

"Because he'd seen the artifacts."

"It must be some treasure," Kruse said, holstering his gun.

"It is."

"Gaines better call in soon. You're his only hope of avoiding the FBI and the Vatican Secret Service."

"He'll call."

"You want me to do anything else while I'm here?"

"No. Get out of there before the FBI shows up. Trying to explain why you and a dead body are at the hideout of the number one fugitive in the world isn't very appealing."

"Gaines and his friend are sitting ducks out there."

"Get a room outside of town. I'll be in touch as soon as we hear from him."

Barbeau left the meeting with the Director shaken. He now knew that this case would likely destroy his career, even if he captured Gaines. But that was the only certainty he could wring out of the ever more bizarre investigation.

The President's involvement was baffling. The Director talked of evidence that the Attorney General had compromised national security on numerous occasions by providing sensitive information to the Vatican Secret Service. Although the average citizen knew nothing about the VSS, within the intelligence community, the elite agency was respected and often utilized. But the VSS was also feared.

The world's oldest, and some said largest, spy network, might not enjoy the enormous budgets that the US, China, Russia, and England spent on espionage, but none of the other agencies could match the Vatican's contacts and access to power. The Church had infiltrated every single government in the world. Some, as in the case of most western countries, with a stunning degree of influence.

Barbeau recalled more of the conversation.

"I'm not trying to *save* my job," the Director had told him. "I'm trying to *do* my job."

"Then, if I'm understanding what you've been telling me, the Attorney General might be corrupt?"

"Yes. That's a possible explanation, or that the Gaines theft could be a case of astonishing historic consequence . . . or both could be true."

"How big is this thing? How deep does it go?"

"I don't know yet. But, for whatever reason, I'm being kept out of the loop and yet allowed to keep my job. It could be to simply preserve me as a scapegoat. It could be because Attorney General Dover wanted to fire me, but the President decided against it."

"But don't you assume Dover was the one who called the President when he changed his mind?"

"No. It could have been anyone."

"But who has that kind of influence?"

"Several members of the cabinet, any number of billionaires, the Pope."

"The Pope? But the President isn't Catholic."

"You don't have to be Catholic to feel the Pope's influence, or his wrath."

"Why would he want to stop the President from firing you?"

"Because the Vatican doesn't want this case to go public. They want Gaines and the artifacts to never have existed. If I get fired, or resign, there will be news about it. As good as the Vatican is at controlling many things, the media is not their strong suit."

"It's not easy to investigate your boss," Barbeau said, motioning to the portrait of the Attorney General that hung beside that of the President's next to the door.

"No, but there are ways. Remember, the Bureau was designed by J. Edgar Hoover. There are secrets and departments within the Bureau that the Attorney General knows nothing about. Hoover created 'DIRT' within the Bureau. Originally the acronym stood for 'Director's Internal Research Trust.' Through the years several of my predecessors expanded and renamed DIRT. Today it stands for 'Director's Internal Recon Team.' It is a completely covert unit that appears on no budgets and operates without even the President's knowledge. The keys pass from Director to Director in a protected tradition."

"Incredible. But why are you telling me?"

"Because DIRT is the only hope we have." The Director's pained expression made Barbeau wonder how much "hope" there was.

"So whom do I trust?" Barbeau asked.

"You trust me, who I tell you to trust, and no one else."

Barbeau nodded. "Okay."

"Going forward, you should assume that nothing is what it seems. You already know Josh Stadler didn't die of heart failure, although we are not allowed to release that information, even to his family. DIRT has confirmed that Vatican agents murdered him using an advanced chemical compound that appears even to most medical professionals as a heart attack. And you know about Atlanta?"

"Dover told me."

"I don't think he told you the whole story, because he doesn't know the whole story. Lambert, the man who was trying to help

Larsen Fretwell escape and died along with everyone else on the catwalk, had an interesting background. His employer is someone you may be familiar with."

Nanski and Leary left Rip's cousin's house about twenty minutes before Kruse arrived. They had stayed long enough only to interrogate Topper. Then Leary said, "Time to send this old man to God for judgment."

He used the same method and drug employed on Josh Stadler. Pisano had wanted them to explore the house thoroughly to locate the papers, but it couldn't be risked. It had already been searched three times before with no luck. The Eysen, obviously still with Gaines, was their singular focus. The hierarchy in Rome suspected Gaines was likely now in possession of the Clastier Papers as well. A greater enemy of the Church could not be imagined, at least not in the earthly realm.

From the house, the helicopter had taken them to a church in Asheville where a car waited. They headed west on I-40 because that's what they expected Gaines to do. The Vatican quietly alerted hundreds of their people to patrol I-40 and nearby secondary roads between North Carolina and Arizona.

"Surely one of the faithful will spot them," Pisano told Nanski. "And then, Gaines and Asher must be apprehended and *dealt* with. However, let me be clear. There is no greater cause in your life than recovering those ungodly objects and getting them to Rome."

Ultimately, finding them along the highways would be a long shot, but the Vatican had a good idea where Gale and Rip might be heading.

37

Saturday evening, a man boarded the Greyhound bus in Greensboro, North Carolina, and asked the old woman sitting next to Sean if she would mind moving.

"I haven't seen my nephew in such a long time," he told her.

As the bus wound through the countryside, the two FBI agents who'd boarded at the stop before, tried to determine the identity of the man now sitting next to Sean. Hall relayed the text messages coming in from the agents, who had managed to get a partial photograph of the guy.

"Who the hell is he?" Barbeau fumed.

"Nothing's coming up in our facial recognition system."

"Do they think Sean Stadler knows the man?"

"Just what I told you. He got on the bus in Greensboro, asked a woman to move, and sat down next to Stadler. They've been talking ever since. Wait a minute . . ." Hall read a message off his phone. "The man has given Stadler earbuds and an iPad. He's showing him something. Our agents can't see what it is."

"Unbelievable!" Barbeau said as he paced to the window of the Asheville Federal Building, looking out into the dimming light as if he might be able to see the bus and determine who the man was. "Arrest them!"

"Sir, that isn't wise. Stadler is our only—"

"I know. Damn it! This joker is interfering with a federal investigation. Get someone in Greensboro to find out where he came from. Run the credit cards, pull surveillance video, figure this out!" Barbeau stormed out of the room to phone the Director.

"I don't know who is on that bus, but are we ready to grab him without Sean Stadler knowing?" the Director asked, frustrated.

"Our two agents on the bus have orders. If he gets off alone along the way, we won't have a problem. If they get off together in Asheville or anywhere else, we'll have to let it play out in order for Stadler to lead us to Gaines."

"The man on the bus could be with the Vatican."

"That's my best guess. If that's true, then we know your boss, the Attorney General, is working on their behalf. No one outside the Bureau knows Sean Stadler is on that bus."

"More bad news. The Governor of North Carolina has called out the National Guard to aid in the search for Gaines."

"Oh, that's going to kill us. Who let that idiot make such a stupid move?"

"I spoke with the Governor a few minutes ago, and he claims the request came from the White House."

"What the hell? Why didn't they consult with us?"

"I've got a call in to the Attorney General's office, but he's at the White House."

"Don't you have Dover's cell number?"

"It went to voicemail."

"Something is so wrong with this picture," Barbeau said.

Sean stared at the iPad in disbelief. For forty minutes the stranger had tried in vain to convince him of something that Sean knew couldn't be true. But now he watched and listened to irrefutable proof of unfathomable crimes and conspiracies. When the video ended, Sean pulled out the earbuds and turned to face the man. The only thing stopping him from crying over what he'd seen was his seething anger.

"What do I need to do?" Sean asked in a gravely whisper.

Rip, agitated, kept checking behind them. "We're too exposed out on the road like this."

"At least this time we're well rested and better equipped," Gale said as rain pounded the windshield of their rental car.

"And we've left an ever-widening trail of destruction behind us. Sean may well have been arrested by now . . . or worse."

They were silent for a few miles. The car was loaded with camping gear, but just after Knoxville the rain had come in torrents.

"Do you really believe it's the Vatican doing all this?" Gale asked.

"They are the only other group who could have known about Clastier's prophecies. They've been waiting centuries for this. Who else would know how important the Eysen is? Who else would have enough at stake to kill so easily? Damn them, Larsen was like a brother to me. I can't believe he's . . ." the words came haltingly, "Dead." Rip groaned. "He wanted me to report the find. If I'd done that a dozen people would still be alive. Those cops in Atlanta had families. They were just doing their job."

"And if you *had* reported it? Who would have it now?"

"I'm not sure the Eysen even works anymore. It's eleven million years old. I don't know how it worked in the first place. But I can tell you that the world has been going along fine for all these years until I dug that thing up."

"Really? Everything's been fine? Humans have been in a constant state of war and genocide. Five hundred million people have died in wars, and another hundred million killed in mass genocides throughout history. Yeah, it's all been fine. Don't even bring up poverty, human-caused disease, slavery, racism, rape, violence, and I could go on and on."

"That justifies my stealing an artifact?" He knew the importance of the Eysen, but the guilt gnawed at him.

"You stealing it is nothing compared to whoever is killing for it. And did you really steal it? Does the US Government own it? Their official version of history makes it impossible for the Eysen to exist. The Eysen doesn't belong to anyone except maybe *you*."

"Me?"

"Clastier sent you a message through his writings to look for it. You did that, and you found it. It belongs to you."

Rip was quiet. He stared out the window for a long time, watching tractor trailers pass as Gale kept close to the speed limit.

"Let's not call Booker," she said, breaking the silence.

"So we can go to Taos to look for some trace of a long-dead priest?"

"A defrocked priest," she reminded. "A man who has guided every step of your adult life."

"Damn it Gale, that's not true. The Clastier Papers are an artifact, like any other. Thousands of artifacts have guided my path, as have any number of other events that have shaped my life – the death of my mother, my failed marriage, meeting—"

"Meeting me?"

"I was going to say meeting Booker Lipton."

"I didn't know your mother was dead."

"Well, she is!" he said, fighting back emotion.

"When did she die?"

"Are you writing a book?" he asked sarcastically.

"Sorry, I can't help it. I'm a reporter."

"No comment."

"So where's your dad?"

Rip sighed. "He's a deejay in Flagstaff."

"On the radio?

"Yeah. What is your problem?"

"Music or talk?"

"Do you ever stop? He's a conservative talk show host. He also does some regular deejay work on an oldies station owned by the same group."

"He's your deceased Asheville uncle's brother?"

"No. My father is an only child."

"So your mother was the descendant?"

"Yeah."

38

"No one killed her, if that's what you're thinking," Rip said. "She had cancer, a very aggressive type. I was fifteen when they diagnosed her. Six months later, she died at home while my father and I held her hands."

"I'm sorry."

"What about your parents?"

"Artists. They run a little gallery in Stowe, Vermont."

"Are you close?"

"Pretty close."

"The FBI has likely visited them. They're probably worried," Rip said.

"Maybe they haven't. Don't you wonder why the media isn't covering our story?"

"They covered Atlanta."

"But we weren't mentioned. No one knows a thing about us."

"That's because they don't want word about the artifacts getting out."

"Exactly," Gale said. "Because someone knows what they are. All the resources they're using to capture us, the Catholic Church, and the silence in the media . . . they know."

"We dug it out of the ground less than a week ago and it's been in our hands ever since. How could they?"

"I don't know. Maybe there's a record of it somewhere."

"An eleven-million-year-old record?"

"Maybe it's not eleven million years old. Maybe it's not the first one that's been found."

Her remark stopped Rip cold.

"Wow. I'll have to think about that. One thing's for sure. We need to spend some time with this Eysen and figure out why it's caused all this trouble. Booker will have a plan. We have to call him. He's our lifeline."

They didn't talk much after that, and drove into the night, switching drivers several times. Rip had borrowed some cash from Topper, but it wouldn't last long. They needed to get to Booker.

Whenever she wasn't driving, Gale read the Clastier Papers. They were a combination of his story, a spiritual guidebook, and predictions for the future. The writings were addictive. She understood how they had captured Rip. He'd been raised on Clastier's words, had much of them memorized. They were an obsession, one he didn't always understand.

"These are pretty esoteric ideas for the 1800s. His philosophies predate even the earliest spiritual or New Age movements by decades. I can see why the Church leaders of his day were annoyed, but why were they so threatened as to hunt him down to destroy his work?"

"It was The Divinations. They were afraid of his predictions for the future."

"Why? Why couldn't they just dismiss him as a heretic? There had to be something else."

"You've read enough of his writings to know he was extremely persuasive and eloquent in his arguments. And yet, at the same time he was a priest and a common man. Quite the force to be reckoned with."

"He says, 'nature is the true church.' Can you imagine? That probably pissed off the Pope," Gale said.

"What about where he claims that the devil exists only in the hearts of men? That the Church just creates external distractions that prevent us from finding the true God within ourselves?"

"Wow. I haven't reached there yet. I guess that's reason enough for a bishop to raise a posse to find him."

"It always struck me that The Divinations were written as fact. As if Clastier had proof these things would happen," Rip said.

"Even the philosophies he espouses are like he positively knew." Gale absently flipped through the pages. "How could he know all this? And about what you would find?"

"As badly as I wanted to find Cosega, I also wanted to know how he knew."

Just after two in the morning, they found a little motel in West Memphis, Arkansas. The rain had been heavy during the whole drive so far, and they were anxious to close their eyes. But first Rip found a payphone and called Booker.

"I can have Kruse there by nine, maybe earlier. He must have just missed you in Asheville," Booker said. "He'll have a new satphone, and we'll get you out of the country. I've got an island off the west coast of Mexico."

"Were those National Guard troops in Asheville for us?"

"Yes. Your little objects have become very important to quite a few, powerful people. And it's going to get worse."

"That's hard to imagine."

"I lost two good men in Atlanta. Rip, there's something else you should know. When Kruse arrived at the Asheville house to pick you up, he found a body."

"What do you mean? Whose?"

"Your neighbor, Topper."

Gale couldn't see the distraught look cover Rip's face, but she heard him moan.

"What is it?" she asked.

Rip didn't answer.

"What?"

"Topper's dead."

"Oh, no. How?"

"How?" Rip asked Booker.

"Don't know. Kruse found him at the top of the stairs, face down. Looks like a heart attack. I'm trying to find out. I'll keep on it."

"They killed him."

"Probably."

"Definitely. The Vatican murdered Topper. They better hope they catch me before I figure out what this thing is. If they're so afraid of it, then it must be able to do some major damage to the Church, that's just what I'm looking to do."

"Stay calm. Sit tight. I want to see this thing. I'll be waiting at the island for you. See you by dinnertime tomorrow."

"Damn them!" Rip exclaimed.

39

Sunday July 16th

Morning came late. The sun remained buried behind a thick ceiling of clouds. The rain hit sideways into the picture window of the $39 motel room, and the parking lot puddled and grayed out of view. It was a misty blur that concealed all but the glow of the Waffle House sign between their room and the highway. There were only five or six channels on the boxy television set. Three of them ran TV ministries seeking cash for salvation, one had news. Rip confirmed there were still no reports of their theft of the artifacts, Larsen's death, or anything connected to their flight.

Gale looked out the window into nothingness. Water poured out of a split gutter above their room, loud and constant.

Rip stared at her blonde curls and then over to his backpack with the Eysen. The dingy motel added to his surreal sense that he was in a B-movie, except that he lacked the requisite karate knowledge, or even a handgun.

The pounding on the door took his breath. He saw the smile fade from Gale's lips. The cruelty of it all overtook her – how had they found them? Was it Barbeau or the Vatican agents? It was way too early for Kruse. There was no time to think. The constant chase had exhausted them.

The pounding came again. "FBI. Open up!" muffled by the metal door and the thundering rain.

As she turned away from the door, Rip already had their packs and was grabbing her arm. She was confused when he led her toward the bathroom. There was no back door and no other windows. She knew they were trapped.

More pounding. How long until they came through the door? Suddenly Rip slid away a small panel above the narrow closet space. He clasped his hands into a stirrup and told her to climb through the opening. He pushed her into the attic crawlspace. It was dark and narrow with musty yellow insulation. She reached down and pulled him up and he quickly replaced the panel. The area was the same size as the room below with concrete firewalls on all sides.

"How do we get out of this?" Gale pleaded, still whispering over the deafening rain pelting the roof.

Pulling his flashlight from his pack, Rip scanned the ceiling searching for a vent, a crack, anything. Then his light revealed a small door below the peak of the roof, and they lunged for it. Rip fiddled with an old rusty barrel-bolt and worked the thick wood open. They wriggled through the tight passage and found themselves in an attic space above the motel room behind theirs. There was only one option.

Rip located the panel to the room on the other side of the building from theirs. Seconds later, they dropped through.

The room was occupied.

"What the hell?" Fischer Carlson said, jumping to his feet. They all stood there for a second staring at each other. Fischer looked seventy-five, but was closer to sixty.

"Sorry to have startled you, but we're kind of in some trouble and we couldn't use the door from our room," Gale explained.

As the word "trouble" escaped her lips, Fischer, already enchanted by her eyes, remembered the color from a childhood dream when he'd been lost on an island. He had been overcome with fear until he came to a place where the sky and the ocean met, merging into that same shade of blue. He had awoken then, so long ago, with an ever-growing ache to search for something, an elusive feeling or place he could never quite identify. In the half-century since, this was the first time he'd seen that color again.

"Where the hell did you come from?" he asked, craning his neck to look up in the ceiling. "Maybe you didn't know, but there's a door in this place."

"We need help," Gale repeated.

"We have to get out of here *now*!" Rip said.

"I have a truck," he said. "If you folks need to move."

Even if there had been another choice, they would have gone with Fischer. Something in his manner made him completely trustworthy. He reminded them both of someone, a close childhood friend neither of them had had.

Gale looked at Rip and back to Fischer. "Please," she said.

In seconds, he gathered some things into an old canvas duffle and followed them out the door into torrential rain. Fischer took the lead. Visibility wasn't more than three feet and they fought the wind. Rip didn't see any evidence of the FBI, and hoped they were still on the other side of the building.

With soaked clothes and dripping faces, they breathlessly climbed into the cab of his semi. He handed them a couple of towels and started the engine.

"I'm Fischer, by the way. Where were you folks wantin' to go?"

40

Leary was drenched when he finally picked the lock and kicked through the chain.

"Where the hell are they?" Nanski shouted once they reached the bathroom.

"They've been here," Leary said, turning off the TV. He pointed to the obviously slept-in bed.

Nanski wiped the rain from his face and tried to think. He looked up to ask for guidance and saw the panel. After closing the front door, Leary pushed him into the attic. Nanski was disappointed not to find them hiding, and devastated once he reached the opening to the other room on the back. By the time he dropped down and ran out into the parking lot, Gale and Rip were well down the road and safe inside Fischer's truck.

Two one-hundred-dollar bills got the grumpy front desk guy to give them the registration information, but "T. Fischer" had paid cash, provided only CA as his plate number, and had listed a post office box in Los Angeles with no zip.

"Aren't you people supposed to get a driver's license number or something?" Nanski asked the befuddled clerk. Leary nudged Nanski and pointed to a state trooper who had just pulled in next to Rip's rental car. "Thanks for your help," Nanski said to the clerk as he peeled off another hundred and handed it to him. "We weren't here, understand?"

The clerk nodded fast. The Vatican agents left the office and walked casually to their vehicle, then headed west on I-40.

A few minutes later, the real FBI joined the state trooper and surrounded the building. After getting the room key from the front desk clerk, who neglected to mention his earlier visitors, agents entered the room and noticed the broken chain lock.

Barbeau, lacking sleep and patience, rallied the strength to not smash his chair through the window of the federal building in Asheville. Instead he pulled out a map.

"We didn't screw up this time," he said to Hall. "We were just late. Maybe only half an hour."

"It's the closest we've been," Hall said.

"Right. And they abandoned their car. Likely they are riding in a truck and heading west."

"Why west?" Hall asked.

"They wouldn't drive back into our arms."

"Unless their trucker's load needed to go east."

Barbeau frowned. Hall was right. "Fine. I want road blocks in both directions."

"It's Sunday. We'll have issues staffing up. If they're in a semi, let's assume they're sticking to the interstates. We've got I-40 east and west and I-55 north and south."

"How quickly can we get them covered?"

"Thirty minutes, tops. Sunday traffic is much lighter. They aren't armed. We've got enough people to do it."

"Shut them down."

Fischer looked over at his passengers, while navigating a wide turn. "Hey, Bonnie and Clyde? Now that we're clear of the motel I'd kinda like to know who's after you."

"It sounds worse than it is," Rip said, regarding the rail-thin, scrappy-looking old man, who appeared to have spent a lifetime behind the wheel.

"It usually does," Fischer laughed. "But my days of being a getaway driver are long past. People don't drop out of my ceiling every day. I'm doin' you a special favor, mostly on account of her bein' too pretty to be dangerous."

"The FBI," Gale said once she caught his glance.

He sniffed in some air and nodded slightly. "What do they think you did? Don't say bank robbery."

"Theft of government property," Rip said.

"You didn't kill no one or nothing?"

Rip thought about Josh, Larsen, and Topper. He had surely killed them, but he knew that wasn't what Fischer meant. "No."

"I got a pickup outside of Little Rock. Is the interstate gonna be a problem?"

"They set up some roadblocks in North Carolina on the interstate yesterday."

Fischer let out a long whistle. Gale could see him considering that information.

"The government property they think y'all took . . . it wasn't from Fort Knox or anything, was it?"

"No," Rip said.

Fischer looked down at the pack Rip clutched in his lap. "And you're sure you didn't rob a bank? 'Cause they get mighty worked up about bank robbers. It's the bankers runnin' things you know?"

"No gold, no cash. We just need to get far away."

"Hmm. Well, I know a back way. It'll take a bit longer."

"We'd appreciate it," Gale said.

Fischer found a place to turn around and headed back in the direction they'd come.

"Are you going to turn us in?" Rip asked after a couple of tense minutes of silence.

Fischer smiled. "Do I look like the turn-folks-in type?"

"Most people wouldn't want to get involved with a couple of fugitives," Gale said.

"I ain't most people." He handed Rip a thermos. "Mind pouring me a cup?"

"Sure."

"The thing is," Fischer began, "this is a bit of a tricky situation. See, I'm on parole."

"So you could get in extra trouble for helping us," Gale said while Rip tried not to spill the coffee.

"Right. So, just for the moment, let's pretend you're caught in my truck. I'm gonna play dumb, like you asked for a ride 'cause your car broke down or something. You never told me you were wanted."

"Of course," Rip agreed, handing him the cup.

"Damn," Fisher said, taking a sip. "It's cold. We're gonna need to risk a coffee stop soon."

"How far are you going?" Gale asked.

"Once I get my load, it's on to San Diego. Where you hoping to go, besides far away from Arkansas?"

"Taos, New Mexico," she answered.

Fischer nodded, as if this made sense.

Rip wished Gale hadn't been so free with their information. They didn't know anything about this guy, and he wasn't even sure they were going to Taos. "How far can you take us?"

"Well, assuming the feds don't catch up to us first and y'all have enough money to buy me a decent meal or two," he said, "I can drop you off in Albuquerque sometime tonight."

Rip mentally calculated his remaining cash.

"You'll drive straight through?" Gale asked.

"Unless one of you can handle this rig." He laughed. "Honey, I got to. I've got an impossible schedule to keep. The only reason you found me at the motel is 'cause I got in too late last night to pick up my load."

Rip hoped they'd get that far, but then what? The only person who could help them had been the only person who had known their location at the motel. Gale was thinking the same thing, but while Rip had a hard time believing that Booker tipped off the FBI, Gale was positive he had.

41

Sean stepped off the bus in Asheville, followed by the man with the iPad. Barbeau and Hall were in radio contact with their agents on the bus, and four more were in cars near the bus station. State and local police were on alert.

"We will not lose this punk again," Barbeau had said half a dozen times. It had been three hours, and the roadblocks on the interstates around West Memphis had yielded nothing other than a minor drug trafficker in the wrong place at the wrong time.

"Targets are getting in a white Lexus," the speaker on the conference table said.

Barbeau paced to the window as if he might be able to look out and see it. "Who is in that car?"

"We don't have an ID," another agent reported.

"Do you have a visual?" Hall asked.

"Affirmative on the visual, negative on the ID. It's not Gaines. Repeat – driver is not Gaines."

"Who the hell is it?" Barbeau asked Hall.

"Follow it," Hall said.

Another agent read off the plate number. Hall fed it into his laptop. "Targets are heading south on Tunnel Road. We are in pursuit."

"Do not apprehend," Barbeau said.

"This is Air One. We have target locked."

Barbeau exhaled, momentarily relaxing knowing that the helicopter had the car in its sights.

It didn't last long.

Hall muted the mic from their end. "The Lexus is a government vehicle."

"Whose government?" Barbeau said. The words stung his lips.

"U.S."

"Unbelievable. What department?"

"Classified."

"Let me see that." Barbeau went to Hall's screen. "Well, we're going to un-classify this little party!"

He dialed the Director.

Nanski and Leary were lucky. They were car number sixty-six in the roadblock, and breezed through before the traffic lines got out of hand. Blindly heading west, they were hopeful that their next encounter with Gaines would end differently.

"Where's your faith?" Leary asked Nanski after noticing him biting his lip in the passenger seat.

"My faith isn't the problem. It's the prophecies."

"I don't get that," Nanski said, popping a breath mint. "So Malachy sees all this going down nine hundred years ago. Shouldn't we have been ready?"

"We've been preparing for this event for many years."

"And if it's prophesized, can it really be changed?" Leary breathed in the minty taste of another candy. "I don't want to be messing with God's plans."

"The Lord has granted us free will. He has given us messages.

We can change it. We *must* change it!" Nanski said impatiently. He was trying to think. The Vatican had some records and reports of Clastier's predictions, The Divinations, but they were far from complete, and now he suspected there was more he hadn't been shown.

Clastier hadn't been hunted because of his Attestations. Those spiritual ideas could be squashed, as had been so many others that disagreed with the Church. But his Divinations corroborated Malachy's prophecies, even though Clastier never knew of them.

"Malachy saw the end of the Church," Nanski said in a dire tone. "And so did others."

"They're all wrong!" Leary said, pounding the dash.

"I pray we'll make them wrong."

He clung to the knowledge that records from Clastier's era were not clear on whether The Divinations meant "end times" or "change times." Without seeing all the writings, Nanski could not be sure if Clastier was referring to the end of the Church, or all of humanity.

They needed his papers, not just to stop their spread, but also to understand them.

"The Director's working on it," Barbeau told Hall. "Meanwhile, we follow this damn car."

"Where could they possibly be going now that Gaines is out of Asheville?"

"Do we *know* he's out of Asheville? All we have is a rental car and an empty motel room. Nobody saw him. Anyone could have taken that car. I honestly don't have the foggiest idea where that son of a bitch is!" Barbeau continued fuming.

"We need to strike the roadblocks in Arkansas. If they're heading west, they could be well past Little Rock. North? South? The circle is too large. We've heard from the governors of

Tennessee, Arkansas, and Missouri complaining about the back-ups."

"No. Tell the governors these are federal highways. I don't care if it takes all day."

"It's going to bring up too many questions."

Barbeau looked at his watch. "Twenty more minutes."

"Targets are now on I-26 south," said a voice from the box.

"Air One, do you still have a visual?"

"Affirmative. They're making it easy. White Lexus traveling the speed limit on a Sunday . . . Sir, Sean Stadler may be heading for the airport."

42

Inside the truck stop, smells of old frying oil and stale cigarettes greeted them. Rip spotted a payphone and debated a call to Booker. He pulled Gale aside while Fischer went to the restroom.

They spoke in hushed tones next to two beeping, unused video games.

"We're in the clear now," Rip said. "We should get out of here before Fischer decides to be a hero."

"We can trust him."

"What makes you so sure?" Rip asked, craning to get a view of the bathroom door.

"Intuition."

"That's not enough."

"What are we supposed to do? Call Booker again? Look what happened the last time. Four hours later, the FBI knocked on our door," Gale said, flashing anger.

"But why would Booker turn us in?"

"I don't need to know that to know we shouldn't call him again. Maybe he didn't turn us in. Maybe they have his phones tapped. But *no one* knows we're with Fischer," Gale said.

"Even if he's not back there calling the cops right now, how long will it take the feds to find out whose room we dropped in on?"

Gale hadn't thought about that. Fischer emerged from the restroom wiping his hands on a brown paper towel when he found them. "Now, about that meal."

They sat by a front window. Semi-trucks moved down the interstate in a never-ending succession, creating a rhythm like waves breaking on the beach. Rip had wanted to get out when they picked up Fischer's load, but they'd been at a deserted warehouse and there was nowhere to go. He had a feeling this might be their last chance. He'd left the casing in the secret room in Asheville and wondered if it had been found by whoever killed poor Topper.

After all these years of protecting the Clastier Papers and looking for what turned out to be the Eysen, it seemed insane that both artifacts, and the Odeon, had wound up in their damp packs at a greasy truck stop in Arkansas. Rip couldn't let go of the circles and their patterns on the casings. If they could be solved, the Eysen might finally reveal its secrets.

"Rip, you sure are lost in thought," Fischer said. He and Gale had been talking, but Rip didn't know what about.

Rip tried to smile, looking at the plate of food that would likely upset his already knotted stomach.

Fischer's weathered face captivated Gale. She wondered what stories each line could tell, sensing a life crafted from the storms and emptiness of decades on the road – and in prison.

"Gale tells me you're an archaeologist."

Rip nodded and shot Gale a look.

"How'd you get into that line of work, other than it makes a great cover for stealing government property?" Fischer winked.

"The past gives us clues as to who we are. Sometimes they are bones, and I try to sense the personality of a long-lost fellow traveler on the journey across time. Those forgotten faces from a distant age laughed and cried. Their experiences, like ours, belong to all humanity. I try to unlock their secrets so that we can hear their stories."

Gale stared at Rip, surprised by his sincere reply.

Four hours later, they blew past Oklahoma City. Four hours after that, they stopped again outside Amarillo, Texas for dinner.

"I've got an old friend in Tucumcari, New Mexico who would probably lend you a car."

"Are you serious?" Gale asked.

"It wouldn't be much. He owes me a few favors. I trust him . . . completely."

"I'm not sure when we could get it back to him."

"Don't worry about that."

Another two hours and they were at a dusty adobe house on the west side of Tucumcari. Fischer's friend, a large, jovial, Hispanic man called Tuke, gave Rip the keys to an old pickup truck. He and Fischer had served time together. "Quite a stretch a number of years back," Fischer told Gale.

"Tuke. That's an unusual name," Gale said.

"My given name is Fernando, but in prison sometimes we pick up other names. Often they call you the name of the town you're from. Tucumcari was too long."

"Tuke, I don't know when, or even if I can get this truck back to you," Rip said.

"I'd kind of like it back, but I'm okay. I owe Fischer. It's on you," Tuke said, looking at Fischer.

Fischer nodded.

Tuke studied his old friend and then nodded in return. "But if you need a place to stay in Taos, I can call a buddy. He's good people."

Gale looked at Rip, who was hesitant, then to Fischer.

"It's a good time to have friends," Fischer said to Gale. "Even if they're borrowed. I learned a long time ago that the loyalty of friends is a greater power than the will of an enemy. A *true* friend will outlast any tangle of trouble and our own desperation."

"Amen," Tuke said. He wrote the name Grinley, along with an address and phone number, on the inside of a partially used pack of matches and handed it to Gale. "I'll call Grinley and tell him you might come 'round."

As Gale and Rip drove away, he noticed tears on her cheeks. "What's wrong?"

"I don't want Fischer to die."

"Why would he die?" Rip asked.

"Because he helped us!" she cried.

Constant thoughts of Josh, Larsen, and Topper haunted him too. They drove on in silent darkness, into the unknown and toward Taos.

43

The white Lexus, carrying Sean Stadler and the man from the bus, along with the driver, stopped at a security gate at the Asheville Regional Airport. The guard had been expecting them and raised the heavy bar, allowing them to pass into the section that housed private planes. A fueled Cessna jet, engines-on, was waiting.

The three men quickly boarded, the tower immediately cleared them for takeoff, and the pilot taxied to the airport's only runway.

Moments later FBI agents stopped at the gate, produced IDs, and demanded the guard raise the gate. The guard refused. An agent jumped the bar and pursued on foot.

"Are they on that plane?" another agent screamed at the guard, pointing to the only aircraft moving. The agent drew his gun. "Open that gate."

The guard refused, but did not draw his weapon.

Another agent arrested and handcuffed the guard while his partner found the button and raised the bar. Simultaneously, back at the Federal building, Hall was talking to air traffic control.

"This is Special Agent Wayne Hall with the Federal Bureau

of Investigation. You have a plane that is preparing for takeoff. You are not to allow it into the air. Do you understand?"

"Uh, yes sir. We do speak English here in North Carolina. But, uh, I'm afraid I can't help you out," the controller said in a country twang.

"Why the hell not? There is a material witness to a federal investigation on that plane!"

"Well, sir, be that as it may, I really don't know if you're truly who you say you are."

"I understand. Can you just delay that takeoff until I can get your boss on the phone? What's the name of your supervisor? I will have the FAA call him and give you authorization."

Barbeau paced behind Hall, dialing the Director on his cell.

"Yeah, well, even if I do believe you, I can't hold this plane."

"You hold that plane until we can reach your supervisor, or you are going to be in a world of trouble. Do you understand? This is the FBI!"

"Cleared for takeoff. I hear you agent, but their authorization comes from a little higher up than yours."

"Listen to me, John-Boy!" Barbeau yelled. "You hold that plane. This is Special Agent Dixon Barbeau, and I'll have the Director of the FBI on your ass in about three minutes."

"You listen to me, *Dick*. If you boys really are FBI, then you sure don't have your act together."

The agents at the airport reported on another line, "It's in the air. Stadler is away."

Hall told the agents to get into that tower and arrest the controller, then went to work trying to obtain a flight plan for the Cessna. Barbeau held his head in his hands and sat back in his chair as if he'd been shot. The Director finally came on the line.

"Barbeau, take me off speaker," he said, and then told him where the order approving the takeoff had originated. Barbeau was stunned, but more of the pieces were falling into place. In his exhausted state, Barbeau knew he needed help to figure this out, yet the Director had told him that no one could be trusted, not even Hall, but he couldn't think of anyone else.

With the FAA tracking the Cessna, and Gaines long gone, Barbeau asked Hall to take a walk with him. They ate take-out sandwiches from a nearby deli on a bench near the street. The air, muggier than normal even for a July night, seemed to hold the light glowing from streetlamps.

"Rain's coming soon," Barbeau said.

It had been an excruciatingly long day. Hall was exhausted, didn't want to talk about the weather, but he knew Barbeau was even worse off. He said nothing.

"This is one screwed-up case. There are some things you don't know, things that aren't in the file, and can't go in the file. Are you good with that?"

"Depends."

"That's not the answer I need."

"Look Barbeau, I don't even like you. I'm not doing something that's going to mess up my career."

"The Director knows everything I'm about to tell you."

"Does he know you're telling me?"

"No."

"Then I don't want to know."

"It's not like that. You know what really happened in Atlanta?" Barbeau asked, not waiting for an answer. "Finn Lambert, one of the suspects killed in the Atlanta catwalk collapse who helped Larsen Fretwell escape the beach in Florida, was ex-CIA."

Hall's interest was piqued. "Where and how did Larsen Fretwell hook up with a spook?"

"That's not all. Lambert's employer at the time of his death was Booker Lipton."

"CIA, Booker Lipton? I'm listening."

"I thought you might be. Turns out Booker funded most of the digs that our Professor Gaines has done."

"That didn't come up on our background searches."

"No," agreed Barbeau. "Booker has taken extraordinary measures to be certain that his support of Gaines, like his employment of Lambert and the other man who died in Atlanta, was not traceable to him."

"Why? Have they been stealing ancient artifacts all these years and running a black market? Does Booker *need* more money?"

"I wish it were that simple. Booker is only a small piece of the puzzle. We have reason to believe that Josh Stadler's murder was ordered by the Vatican and carried out by its agents."

"Whoa!" Hall said. "I thought the Vatican only did straight intelligence. I didn't think they did murder, at least not in the last hundred years or more."

"It's unusual, but not uncommon. They normally have much cleaner ways to advance their agenda, given the Church's vast reach and influence."

"The artifacts must have some pretty amazing religious significance," Hall said.

"Oh, the artifacts are *very* significant," Barbeau replied. "Those same agents are probably the ones who beat us to Gaines in the West Memphis motel. They may even have him now."

"Goddamn."

"And you want to talk about a significant artifact? Remember what the air traffic controller said? Someone with more juice than the FBI ordered that plane into the air. Well, let me tell you that the people who just helped Sean Stadler escape work for the NSA."

"Barbeau, I thought I said I didn't want to know."

"Wait, I haven't even told you about the White House," Barbeau said coolly.

Hall walked to a trashcan to dump his food wrappers, but kept his soda. "Tell me about the White House," he said, returning.

"That's the part we know the least about," admitted Barbeau, "but the Attorney General seems to be coordinating the investigation with the Vatican. The President has knowledge of the arrangement, thereby giving tacit approval."

"Let me see if I've got this straight. The Catholic Church is dictating the actions and the resources of US law enforcement at its highest levels?" Hall asked, skeptically.

"Correct."

"What else are they controlling? What other policy decisions are they making for us?"

"It's hard to say how big this is," Barbeau said.

"Back up. You said the NSA was involved. Are they monitoring the Vatican, or the Bureau?"

"Come on, you know they monitor *everything*. Their interest in this case seems to be related to one of the artifacts. They either want it, for some reason known only to them, or they are simply trying to keep it out of the Vatican's hands."

"Why do they want a couple of stone bowls, and . . . hold on a minute. They aren't stone bowls," Hall said, standing back up and pacing in front of the bench. "The photos and witnesses say it was a globe that they pulled out of the cliff. A *hollow* globe. Those casings were protecting something. This isn't about the casings or the little quartz oval artifact at all. Something was inside, and Gaines took it with him. That's why he so easily sent one of the casings away, because it's just a damn wrapper for the real prize."

"The globe is like a Trojan Horse," Barbeau said. "We've had people working day and night trying to decode the carvings on the casing with absolutely no luck. We've been so focused on what the outside was that it never occurred to me, or anyone else apparently, that the important thing was inside."

"But what was so vital to get the Vatican committing murder and the NSA stomping all over the FBI?"

44

Monday July 17th

In Tuke's old pickup, Gale and Rip stayed on back roads and encountered few cars. Around two in the morning, just outside Taos, they drove down a narrow dirt Forest Service road, pulled over, and fell asleep in the truck. They were awakened by a sharp knock on the driver's side window. A forest ranger motioned for Rip to roll down the window. He silently cursed himself for being there, glanced around looking for an escape, then complied.

"Sorry, sir. The trip from Amarillo took longer than we expected and, a few hours ago we realized we were too tired to drive any farther," Rip explained to the ranger.

"Where are you heading?"

"Taos."

"You've only got about twenty more minutes to go. Are you okay to drive now?"

"Yes, sir. Thanks."

"Okay," he said, nodding to Gale. "Sleeping is only allowed in designated camping areas within the Carson National Forest." The ranger waved them on.

"That was close," Gale said as they drove away.

"I kept thinking he was going to ask for ID," Rip said. "Let's get something to eat and then head to Grinley's place. We'd be crazy to spend one more minute on the road."

"I thought you weren't sure about Fischer and his friends?"

"If he was going to turn us in he'd have done it by now. I think your instincts are right about him. Besides, right now his crowd is on the same side of the law we are. I think I feel better with them."

Gale ran into Cid's Food Market for supplies, and they gobbled sandwiches as they headed north. She wanted to visit the Taos Pueblo, Clastier's last stop before fleeing, but knew Rip was right. They needed to get off the road. The town had the feel of another country, with adobe houses built of mud and straw nestled against the Sangre de Cristo Mountains.

Rip slowed down as they crossed the Gorge Bridge. A straight, six hundred-foot drop down the narrow canyon to the Rio Grande River – terrifying in its beauty – made it a popular spot for suicide jumpers. The bridge was the final landmark before the turnoff to a winding dirt road.

Fifteen minutes later, they pulled into Grinley's driveway. The house wasn't visible from the road, but a large, barking, golden-colored dog escorted them the remainder of the way.

The place may have been one of the oddest structures Rip had ever encountered, or at least it was in the western hemisphere. Part adobe, part log cabin, with some kind of corrugated metal spaceship-type siding. On top of that there were castle-like turrets lining the edges of the roof, as well as towers on the corners.

Gale and Rip remained in the car for several minutes, less worried about the dog than the outlandish dwelling in front of them. Finally, a shirtless man with thin, shoulder-length gray hair and a matching scraggly beard appeared at the front door.

Rip thought he saw him set down a shotgun on the front porch.

"Who sent ya?" the wiry, tanned man asked.

"Tuke," Rip answered, opening the car door. "I'm Rip. This is Gale."

"Thought so," he said, his eyes darting about, sizing up the strange people from the civilized world. "Do you like prickly pear salad?"

Gale smiled. "You must be Grinley?"

"To some folks."

"You're kind to have us."

"I'm partial to those that piss off *The Man*," Grinley said.

"We've managed to do that," Rip said, glad his misfortune was at least good for something.

A rabbit ran out of the trees, and not far behind was a big gold dog. "That Deeohjee, he's always gettin' after bunnies." Grinley shouted, "Git 'em, boy!"

"Deeohjee, what an unusual name. How do you spell it?" Gale asked.

Grinley smiled. "D – O – G". Then he erupted in laughter. "Come on in."

Inside, sun from a large skylight filtered through blown glass tubes and bulbs of every imaginable shape and color. Grinley motioned as Gale marveled.

"An old girlfriend did those. Everyone in Taos is an artist, or at least knows one."

Rip didn't have much patience left. He had waited days to get back to the Eysen, desperate to unravel its mysteries. A brilliant plan was needed for staying one step ahead of their pursuers, but what Grinley said next grabbed all his attention.

"Just saw your photo on CNN.com. They say you killed a man."

45

Rip, stunned by the news, turned so quickly his head caught a protruding log and he started to fall before Grinley caught him.

"Are you okay?" Gale asked as Grinley got Rip into a large, plush, leather chair.

"Hell no. Now I'm wanted for murder. Can you show me the story?" Rip asked, trying to get up.

"I'll bring you my laptop. Sit tight."

"Thanks. I know you have no reason to believe me, but I *didn't* kill anyone."

"I know you didn't," Grinley said, handing him the computer. "I could tell when I first looked at you that you hadn't."

"How can you be sure?" Gale asked.

"Because once you've killed a person, you can recognize the look on someone else's face."

Gale stared at Grinley.

"Don't worry, I haven't done it often. Or lately."

"Were you a soldier?" Gale asked, unable to suppress her reporter's curiosity.

"You might say I was a soldier in the war on drugs." He laughed.

"I can't believe this. Gale, they're saying I'm the prime

suspect in lab technician Ian Sweedler's death. Those bastards killed Ian and they're blaming *me*! Why would they kill Ian?"

"Because he saw the casing," Gale said.

"Are they going to kill the students next?"

She shuddered. "I wouldn't put it past them. But Ian was different. He was an expert on ancient artifacts. He got a good look at the casing and probably recorded details. If Ian went public, he would have been believed."

"Yeah," Rip said, testing the bump on his head. "Josh, Larsen, Topper, Ian, Booker's guy, those cops in Atlanta . . . there's a trail of blood behind us."

He looked up at Gale, hoping her eyes would forgive him. Instead they nearly broke him. He covered his mouth and fought tears.

"You want some ice for your head?"

Rip didn't answer.

"Maybe some smoke?" Grinley held up a small, carved, wooden box and flipped the lid open, revealing at least ten ounces of pot.

"No, thanks," Gale said.

"What we really need is to do some work. Is there somewhere private we can work? In the sun?"

Grinley led them through the maze of a house, filled by plush leather chairs and couches, carved wooden tables, and beautiful paintings. They passed several black metal spiral staircases leading to the roof.

"Quite a place," Gale said.

"A big-time drug lord built it in the early seventies. Taos was a kind of Wild West back then – hippies, dropouts, mercenaries, fugitives, crazies." He laughed. "I guess it hasn't changed much!"

"Were you here, back then?"

"Oh yeah, as best as I can recall. I came here as a runaway in seventy-two. I was sixteen. Worked for Trog. He's the one who built this place."

"How'd you wind up with it?"

"You'll have to excuse Gale, she's a reporter," Rip said, emphasizing the word "reporter" as if he were saying "Nazi."

"I don't mind. I've got nothing to hide except a whole bunch of stuff I don't want the cops to know about," Grinley said, opening a door into a courtyard surrounded by the house. It was about thirty by thirty square feet with a fountain, in the center was an odd bronze sculpture of a naked, blindfolded woman, holding dozens of scales of justice. But it was the sea of six-foot-high marijuana plants filling the space that made Gale laugh.

"Yeah, you have nothing to hide," Gale said.

"Oh, this?" Grinley waved a dismissive hand. "Pot is practically legal in Taos. Sunny enough for you Rip?"

"Perfect. Thank you."

"I'll leave you to it then," Grinley said, heading back inside. "I'm just going to check online and see how much of a reward I'll get for turning you in."

He wandered into the house laughing.

"He's not going to turn us in," Gale said.

"Maybe he should before someone else gets killed."

"Listen to me." Gale grabbed his shoulders and looked into his eyes. The blue irises caught the bright sun and took his breath away. "Each death confirms that we did the right thing. It's not the other way around. They can kill two hundred people and it'll just make me want to run faster, farther. Do you not understand that?"

"The first time I met Josh was also the last time I met him. And Larsen was my closest friend—"

"Stop torturing yourself. You've been looking for this your whole life."

"No. Not this. I was looking for something to prove my theory. This is something that *disproves* everything we've ever known. This little prize gets everyone who finds out about it killed," he said, pulling the Eysen from his pack.

The lights started glowing immediately. They sat down on

the thick cushions of the heavy metal patio chairs, their knees touching.

"It must get its power from the sun, but I don't see any collectors. How does it do that?" Gale asked, not expecting an answer as the Eysen went through its now familiar spinning-earth sequence.

"No idea. I'm just glad it's working again," Rip said, looking over his shoulder to check if Grinley was around.

The image abruptly switched to a view of a large black globe with millions of pinpoint crystals covering it. They marveled as hundreds of layers were revealed, one after the other.

"It seems to be showing us the composition and construction of the Eysen," Rip whispered.

"Like it heard what I asked," Gale said, stunned.

"Do you think it's interactive somehow?" Rip asked, almost to himself.

The Eysen filled with golden flowers.

"I think it just answered yes!" Gale laughed.

46

Sean Stadler and the man from the bus, whom Sean had heard called "Jaeger," ate breakfast on a secluded deck. The driver of the white Lexus in Asheville and another NSA "specialist" were in the front room of the large log cabin. A third patrolled the grounds. The Cessna had landed the previous night at the Angel Fire Airport in New Mexico. At 8,600 feet above sea level, its two runways were among the highest in the United States. The pilot had warned it might be a tricky landing, but everything went smoothly.

Fifteen minutes after touching down, they were at an NSA safe house nestled in the ponderosa pine forests of the Sangre de Cristos Mountains, twenty-five minutes east of Taos.

Now they waited. Sean needed to get to Gale and Rip – there were warnings to convey and so many things to discuss. The NSA had been meticulous in this case, and was narrowing down Gaines' location with each passing hour.

They knew the Vatican's suspicion, that the fugitives would head to Taos, in the same way they learned most everything – by intercepting phone calls and email transmissions. In this instance they'd seen the photos shared between Pisano and the Cardinal in Rome and had heard their conversations. They even had the information that had passed from Attorney General Dover to the Vatican, and noted that the Pope's representatives had not reciprocated with any of their own information. Dover didn't know about Taos, didn't have a clue about the Eysen, but the NSA most certainly did.

The secret committee which dictated NSA's tasks, had given a "Scorch And Burn" or "SAB" directive. It was only the third such order ever. The second had concerned Edward Snowden's leaks, and the first, no one left alive outside the committee knew.

And now the third SAB had been issued about the Eysen.

Jaeger knew that an SAB meant nothing was out of bounds – breaking laws, assassination – whatever it took to achieve the objective, to get the Eysen. Most people didn't know that the NSA, an agency so secret that is had once been called "No Such Agency," even had agents. The fact was that since 2001 the NSA had developed a huge secret force, which was unequaled in power and resources.

As he walked in, Hall tossed Barbeau a bag of almond croissants. Barbeau pulled one out and flashed a rare smile, but then launched into a rant. "The NSA scoops up our best lead and we can't even find out where they've taken him. I've been on with the Director twice already this morning and he says we're getting stonewalled on both sides. The Attorney General and NSA both have seemingly opposing goals, and we're stuck trying to arrest this guy before one of them kills him."

"I was up half the night trying to figure out what the hell was inside those casings," Hall said. "It's impossible to imagine anything dug out of the ground that the NSA would need so badly."

"We found Ian Sweedler's body an hour ago in a wooded lot

not three-quarters of a mile from his lab. Like the killer wanted it to be discovered."

"Who did it?"

"Had to be the Vatican."

"Why?" Hall asked.

"Don't you see the pattern? Anyone connected to the casings is dead or missing."

"Damn it. We need answers," Hall said.

He and Barbeau had talked until well past eleven the previous night and had developed a new structure. Hall would run the Booker side of the investigation, which included Gaines, Asher, and Larsen Fretwell. Barbeau would focus on the NSA, the Vatican, Sweedler, and the Stadler brothers. The Director's deep-unit, known as "DIRT," consisting of hand-picked, trusted agents would work the high-level stuff, including the connections among the Attorney General, the Vatican, and the President. DIRT also provided their best hope for any insights into the NSA. They all had scrambled phones to protect against NSA eavesdropping, including Barbeau and Hall, but it came down to who had the latest and greatest technology. Hall was betting on the NSA.

"We need to figure out what the NSA is doing with Sean. I mean, how much could he know?" Hall asked.

"Yeah. He didn't even know Gaines or Asher before he picked them up on the parkway. They only spent twenty-four hours together, but the NSA hears all the calls and they must know, or think, that Sean can lead them to Gaines."

"Why don't we find the Vatican agents and follow them? They seem to be a step ahead of us."

"The Attorney General is making sure they're ahead," Barbeau said, disgusted.

"Because he's a Catholic? Or is there something else?"

"He's seriously Catholic. I've never met a man with a deeper faith who doesn't wear a collar."

"Then explain the President. He's taking a risk giving the AG this much room. Laws are breaking all over the place and it's coming from the Justice Department."

"Those laws don't apply anymore," Barbeau said. "If it's under Homeland Security, there are ways to get anything done."

"Yeah, but our hands are tied."

"For the moment. But the Director is working on it."

"He may not survive this," Hall said.

"He doesn't care if they fire him."

"I'm not talking about being fired."

47

Nanski and Leary had left their Albuquerque hotel room just after dawn, picked up a fast food breakfast in Española, and had driven straight to Ranchos de Taos. The tiny town, a few miles south of Taos, was home to the famous San Francisco de Asis Mission Church. Leary parked across the plaza, pumped a mint spray into his mouth, and walked around the exterior while Nanski went inside.

The beautiful adobe building, constructed between 1772 and 1816, had been the subject of paintings by Georgia O'Keefe and photographs by Ansel Adams. It housed the legendary "Shadow of the Cross," a life-sized painting of Christ done in 1896 by Henri Ault, that inexplicably glowed in the dark.

But Nanski and Leary weren't interested in the architecture or the miraculous painting. They were there to greet Gaines who, they felt sure, would arrive soon. Although expunged from Church records and lost to history, Father Clastier had once regularly preached at San Francisco de Asis.

"If Gaines is coming to Taos," Nanski had told Leary, "the only reason is to seek out Clastier, and this Church is where he must begin."

Nanski came out of the church smiling. "Gaines hasn't been here yet."

"You're sure he'll come?" Leary asked. "Why would he risk it?"

"He'll come. I just don't know how long it will take. He is the last true follower of the great heretic." Nanski's phone rang. It was Pisano. After the call, he told Leary, "More good news. They are about to formally charge Gaines with the murder of the lab technician. It'll hit the media in about ten minutes."

"Good. That should help flush him out," Leary said.

"Absolutely. His time is short and God is on our side. Another gift we have received. Do you recall the copy of Thomas Aquinas' *On Being and Essence* that we found at Gale Asher's place?"

"Of course. It was lovingly inscribed by Senator Monroe."

"Yes. Pisano met with the Senator today. It seems that back when Monroe was still an unmarried college professor at Georgetown, he had an affair with his favorite student, Gale Asher. They are still very close."

"The Lord works in mysterious ways," Leary said, smiling. "Do you think that Gaines has any idea his partner in crime has a deeply personal relationship with the most important Catholic in the country?"

"And likely the next American President," Nanski added.

Leary laughed. "I'll bet Ms. Asher has kept that bit her little secret."

Barbeau looked at his phone. "It's the Director. He's calling early," he said to Hall.

"It's getting messy," the Director began. "The Attorney General just announced murder charges against Gaines. He's on all the cable news channels."

"For whose murder?" Barbeau shot back.

"Ian Sweedler."

"Impossible. Dover knows that's BS," Barbeau said.

"Of course he knows, but we've been completely circum-vented. It all came out of the Justice Department. The Attorney General didn't ask me because he knew what I'd say. Hell, we found the body only an hour ago," the Director explained.

"Someone's getting nervous."

"I'm sure they are. *I* am. Aren't you nervous? Why haven't we caught this guy?"

"Sir, with all due respect," Barbeau said, "part of the blame for our failure rests with the fact that the Justice Department, NSA, and White House are all working against us."

"Even though the hand we've been dealt is garbage, we still have to play the game."

"Understood."

"Good. And we did catch a break. DIRT has identified two of the Vatican agents. One of them used his credit card yesterday to get gas on I-40 twice, and again last night to pay for a hotel room in Albuquerque," the Director said.

Barbeau covered his phone and shouted across the room, "Hall, get us on the first flight to Albuquerque."

"I've emailed you their files," the Director continued. "Mark Leary and Joe Nanski. These guys are likely the ones who killed Josh Stadler, and maybe even Ian Sweedler."

"They sound like a couple of real Christians."

"Not the first people to kill in the name of God."

Booker's man, Kruse, had arrived at the motel in West Memphis an hour after the FBI. He watched from a safe distance as agents collected evidence and interviewed potential witnesses. After conferring with an unhappy Booker, Kruse headed to Little Rock and got a room near the airport. He waited, reading one of his preferred dystopian novels, and was engrossed in the final pages of Hugh Howey's *Wool* when Booker called with an update.

"My sources say Albuquerque. One of my jets is already on its way. Your flight leaves in ninety minutes."

Kruse liked traveling by private jet, and enjoyed being able to take his guns and other weapons of choice anywhere in the world. "What's the plan?"

"Hopefully we'll know more by the time you get there. And Kruse, if we do get another chance, you *can't* miss him this time."

48

Gale and Rip watched the Eysen for hours, its mysteries and complexities seeming only to multiply. Most of the images were moving like a video, and almost exclusively were depictions of nature. The one showing a breakdown of how the Eysen was constructed had indicated a technological sophistication beyond humanity's current level.

Other than the rotating Earth routine, the sequence had changed. The only repeat was of the Crying Man, the portrayal so life-like they had to continually remind themselves that he was not actually inside the Eysen. Sometimes it seemed as though the Eysen responded to their questions, even their thoughts, but the concept was so utterly outlandish that even when it appeared to react to them, they shook their heads in disbelief.

"There he is again," Gale said as the Crying Man materialized out of an ocean storm. Other than an occasional sea of faces, he was the only human they'd seen. "Why is he so sad?"

The Crying Man opened his arms. His own Eysen material-ized before him and grew so that they could not tell the differ-ence between theirs and his. The Earth image, with its different arrangement of continents, came through. Sporadic lights covered the landmasses, as if seen from a nighttime satellite image.

"They're like glowing jewels scattered on the ground," Gale said.

"Yes, but look. They are not like our cities built along the coasts. There are almost no lights there. They built their cities inland."

Rip realized he'd said, "*they built*," and paused, trying to recall when he had decided that they were an identifiable group. *They* had built cities, the Eysen, and who knew what other remarkable things. Who were they? What happened to them?

The Eysen drew him back from his thoughts as the lights of "cities" intensified and then went suddenly dark.

"What happened?" Gale asked

Rip stared silently into the dark Eysen. The Crying Man returned.

"Did they destroy their civilization somehow? Is that what we just saw?" Gale asked.

The Eysen filled with yellow flowers. Rip looked at Gale.

"I know it's impossible, but I really think it's answering us," she said.

"It's not completely impossible. Artificial Intelligence may one day get this far. Maybe time is like a loop. Maybe it's already gotten there once."

The flowers, moving slowly, remained.

"Rip, if this really is millions of years old, how did it survive when nothing else of their civilization did?"

"Because they wanted us to find this." His own answer surprised him. "Don't you see? They left it for us."

The flowers multiplied until it looked as if they would crack the Eysen from within and explode out into the dwindling sun of the current day.

"Wait a minute," Rip began. "Maybe it can tell us what the casing's carvings mean."

The images quickly shifted to thousands of circles, lines, and stacked dashes. The sequence continued impossibly fast. Circles turned to planets and orbits, then to rings in a tree, then back to circles. The rapid display must have shown a million images in a second. It was so dizzying that Gale had to turn away. Rip fought nausea and continued watching.

The image suddenly stopped on a view of the casing which had enclosed the Eysen, only now it appeared as if the casings were inside the Eysen. Each carved symbol from the "stone bowls" appeared magnified, and synched with the planetary movements.

It took nearly an hour before Rip yelled out, "Cosega! It really is Cosega!"

"What?" Gale asked.

"This part of the Cosega Sequence not only showed me what the carvings mean – at least some of them – it *proves* the Cosega Theory. Humans not only lived on earth millions of years ago, but they had an advanced civilization far beyond what our craziest science–fiction writers dream of today."

"How did the Cosega Sequence tell you all that? What do the carvings mean?"

"They're a numbering system. Simple really. The dots represent one trip for Earth around the sun – a year. A single circle is ten years, two circles inside each other are a hundred, three a thousand, and so on until the circles with five circles inside, being six, are a million, and nine circles are a billion."

Gale stared at him, speechless. Finally she whispered, "I can't believe you figured it out."

Rip smiled. "I've barely scratched the surface, but of this I'm sure. The Cosega Sequence starts more than four point five billion years ago with the very creation of Earth, and follows it through to when the casing and Eysen were made, *by humans*, more than eleven million years ago!"

"It's our proof of age?" Gale asked excitedly. "We know how old the Eysen is?"

"It's proof of *everything*."

49

The Eysen was more addictive than ever. The Cosega Sequence continued to provide a tour of the planet's history that was far different than what science considered truth, yet Gale and Rip both sensed there was another layer to the Cosega Sequence that might provide even more inconceivable details.

"Looks like we're about to get a storm," Gale said.

Rip looked up at the threatening clouds. "Okay, this might be a good time to take a break." He reluctantly wrapped the Eysen and slid it into his pack.

The winds picked up with the darkening sky. Grinley appeared, along with the first raindrops.

"Time for our daily monsoon," he said. "Usually only lasts forty-five minutes or so. This one looks a bit meaner."

Gale and Rip followed him inside. They hadn't eaten since breakfast and asked to use the kitchen. Grinley led them to another side of the house to a room with a full south-facing wall of slanted glass, filled with plants and vegetables growing in the sun. The kitchen was a funky arrangement of handmade cabinets topped with rough stone slabs. Gale unpacked groceries while Rip started making sandwiches.

"I'm not the questioning type normally," Grinley began, "but you two aren't particularly the criminal type. So maybe—"

"Look, we appreciate you taking us in, but I think not being the questioning type is better for all of us," Rip said. "Are you hungry?"

Grinley's face tightened, offended. "You don't mind taking my shelter. I'm not exactly a boy scout here. If the authorities show up looking for you, I'm likely to suffer as much as you."

Gale feared he'd be killed. "What Rip so gruffly said, doesn't begin to express our gratitude. You and your friends have found us in the midst of a truly desperate situation, and you've saved us." Her eyes disarmed him as they had so many others.

"We're on the same side of the heavy-handed law Gale. In times of trouble, I've often found that the ones called criminals are the only ones you can count on. Everyone else has too much to lose."

Gale smiled and handed him a sandwich.

"I'm sorry Grinley." Rip said. "Gale is right. We owe you a great deal, and an explanation is the least we can do."

"Rip didn't kill that man. He was actually a friend of his," Gale said.

Grinley nodded.

"You probably read online that I'm an archaeologist," Rip said. "We found something on a dig in Virginia that is very important and threatening too many powerful people. They don't mind killing to get it."

"Do you have it with you?"

Rip didn't want to answer, but he knew Gale would, and better it come from him. "Yes."

"Can I see it?"

"Everyone who has seen it is dead," Rip said.

"They've killed at least four people that we know of already," Gale added.

"You don't want to see it," Rip warned.

Grinley stared at him for a long moment. Rip didn't know if he was going to rob him, shoot him, or kick him out.

"Okay." He nodded to Gale. "Damn good sandwich."

They ate and talked about things other than the Eysen and the authorities. Grinley told stories of his decades in Taos, the strange house, and even some tales from prison. Gale and Rip relived various adventures around the world as the rain stormed on for several hours. By the time it stopped, Rip was asleep on the couch, Grinley had vanished into another part of the house, and Gale had jumped back into the Clastier Papers. She wondered about the originals and the casing left in the secret room back in Asheville. If the Vatican agents were responsible for killing Topper, surely they had ransacked the place and found the hidden treasures by now.

Rip awoke thinking back to the first time, as a teen in Asheville, North Carolina, that he'd read Clastier.

Buried deep, a miniature planet spins black within a stone-hard exterior, which once illuminated will forever alter all that is known. We have ridden the movement of lands while great kingdoms filled with dreams. Flight and power have risen and fallen over and over. The turmoil of time has left us lost in this grand cycle, not realizing we have been here before, not understanding that we are not the first to start down this path.

This can be found because it is meant to be found. The cost may be large, for even now opposition is growing against this quest, but it is there. They left it for you. If the search is true, one could rip gains, treasures of every form, and all the profound answers from that which is lost.

The words, written almost two hundred years earlier, were seemingly meant for him, a version of his name even concealed within The Divination. But he'd always considered that a coincidence. When Gale first read it, she screamed. She was convinced that "rip gains" had been a mistranslation of his name and wanted to go back to Asheville to get the original to prove it.

The Divination seemed to foretell the discovery of the Eysen. Although long before he found what he was looking for, he had decided that the physical form it took wouldn't matter. He would know it when he found it. It may have been those passages that drove Rip to spend his life searching, but the complete Clastier Papers captivated him long before he'd even reached that part.

50

Rip couldn't keep his eyes open and fell back asleep for almost an hour. This time he woke from a dream screaming, "Run, run, run!"

"It's okay. We're safe," Gale said from a few feet away. "We're in Taos. No one knows where we are."

"They do," he said, still agitated. "Oh." He took an involuntary deep breath. "Was it just a nightmare? Hundreds of people with guns were after us."

"We're safe," she repeated.

"For how long? They'll keep hunting and they'll find us."

"People can stay hidden for years."

"Not people like us. Not people they want this bad."

"Clastier will help us."

Rip pulled himself up. "How?"

"I don't know. But I believe that's why we're here."

"Did you think we were going to show up in Taos and someone would meet us in the Plaza and say, 'Oh, you're here to see Clastier? He's waiting for you. Right this way.' Is that something you thought could happen?"

"I don't know what I thought, but I'll tell you this. I'm a journalist. I write stories, and they all have a beginning, a middle, and an end. Sometimes the ending takes a while to find. But our story, the one about Clastier and the Eysen, is going to end right here in Taos where it all began."

"Why? Why can't it end in Wichita, or Africa, or the mountains of Virginia where it really began eleven million years ago?"

"Because Clastier was the first one to write it down."

"Was he? What about the Crying Man? What about the other faces in the Eysen? What did they have to say? They wrote in their own way, using the only method they could be sure we would understand millions of years later – images!"

"But surely you see the connections Rip? You are one of the only remaining people who even knows about Clastier. You have his papers. You found the Eysen. The Catholic Church has killed to suppress Clastier's Papers and the Virginia artifacts. The Divinations . . . there are no coincidences."

"Of course. I know. But I also understand that Clastier is *dead.*"

"I can't believe you are saying that. You're one of the great archaeologists. You've spent your whole career communicating with the dead. All those artifacts bring the past alive again. This is no different." She stood up and grabbed the translated pages. "We need to be where Clastier lived and learned. Taos is like one giant dig site. There are clues here that can help us unravel this mystery. It's our only hope to survive. I'm a reporter, you're an archaeologist. We can do this!"

"You're right," he said, nodding his head slowly as if he suddenly understood what they needed to do.

"I'm right?"

Rip stood and looked directly into those eyes that he had so often tried to avoid, but just as often had distracted him. He braved the blueness and the depth of them.

"Clastier knew about the Eysen. It seems impossible, but somehow he knew."

Grinley fixed a southwestern style dinner of vegetarian burritos, chips and salsa with guacamole, green chili stew, and a grilled prickly pear salad. He refused any attempts to help, and insisted they tell him more stories of their travels and adventures prior to becoming fugitives.

Grinley had smuggled drugs into and out of Mexico for years in his youth. He still did a substantial business in marijuana sales, but avoided the chemical and refined drugs currently so popular on the streets. Rip found himself genuinely fond of the old guy, and he didn't often take to people much. He could see Gale also adored Grinley, but she loved everyone.

The three of them laughed well past dinner. Gale had never seen Rip so relaxed and human. She could tell that Grinley enjoyed having company and reveled that they were "outlaws."

"Grinley, can we stay here for a while and study what we found?" Gale asked.

Rip looked at her, surprised.

"We've managed to lose our pursuers," she said to both of them. "No one has a clue where we are. We're about as far off the map as you can get and still be in the US. All we need is a little time to figure it out."

"Figure out what you found? Or what to do next?" Grinley asked.

"Both."

"I'll tell you what. Y'all can stay here a spell, and if it gets too hot for either of us I'll help you get out of the country."

"Where to?" Rip asked, interested.

"Mexico. From there, almost anywhere you want in Central or South America."

"Really?" Rip asked. "We'll never get across the border."

"Ha! Gettin' into Mexico is a whole lot easier than gettin' into the US. There's routes 'cross the desert. It won't be a problem. The farther south you go, the easier it is getting into and out of the smaller countries. I've got friends who have disappeared. It's not as hard as you think."

"Fate was kind to us Grinley, delivering us to your door," Gale said, giving him a hug.

"Fate? I thought it was Tuke I had to blame for this intrusion," he said with a wink. "Tuke always was good at getting me into trouble. Even in prison that crumb could find the rattlers in a box of worms. When we were in federal prison in Tucson he got this guard to . . ."

The story lasted twenty minutes, and by the end Rip's eyes were heavy and his body exhausted. He was still catching up on sleep.

Gale and Rip shared a room with twin beds. Once alone, they talked quietly.

There was a plan now. Grinley could be trusted. The Eysen's age had been confirmed, their pursuers eluded, and they had a safe place to continue to study the artifacts.

"We even have a back-up plan to leave the country," Gale said, as she turned out the light. "Let's get some sleep. I have a feeling great discoveries await us tomorrow."

A few minutes passed before he answered.

"I'm not sure how, but maybe we've actually done it. Somehow, surviving the past week while all that power aligned against us, makes me believe that Clastier was right," Rip whispered in the darkness.

"About what?"

"Changing the world."

"He was. We're going to do it," Gale said sleepily.

They slept for eight solid hours, not moving, not dreaming, just deep in a slumber that their bodies seemed to sense would have to last them a while.

In the days to come, sleep would be rare.

51

Tuesday July 18th

Gale and Rip sat in the courtyard, waiting as the sun rose high enough to hit the Eysen. Wrapped in Mexican blankets against the chill of the high desert dawn, sipping tea, they were silent until the Earth part of the Cosega Sequence completed.

"It's really a computer!" Gale said as the Eysen clicked through a review of everything it had shown them up until that point. "We have an eleven-million-year-old computer."

"Can you imagine what it can tell us?" Rip asked. "If we can stay alive long enough to figure out how to use it that is"

"They don't have any idea where we are." She waved her hand. "This old house is in the middle of dusty-nowhere."

"I know, but—"

"Don't worry so much. We're good."

"Following some drug smuggling route into Mexico doesn't sound good to me."

"Then when we decide to leave we'll find some out-of-the-way motel in the Colorado mountains. Or we'll get to Nevada. We can get lost in that wasteland for sure. There are places."

"And you think we can just disappear and study away?" Rip

felt okay the night before, but he'd awakened worried again. "Do you really think they'll just let us get away?"

"You can only find what you can find. They haven't caught up to us yet, and now we've left no trace. We can do it Rip."

"Or we could get to Booker. He could get us anywhere in the world. That man can hide things."

"It's not worth the risk. I know you trust him, but there is so much you don't know about him. Booker was your friend and supporter when he wanted something from you."

"What did he want?"

"The Eysen."

"No one knew this thing even existed."

"Booker knew something. Why would one of the world's richest men decide to sponsor an endless series of archaeological digs?"

"He loves archaeology. He's interested in the past."

"Come on."

"You're paranoid."

"I'm a reporter."

"Then how did he know?"

"You said there are missing Clastier Papers."

"That was always the rumor."

"Maybe Booker has them."

"And they give details about the Eysen?"

"Maybe. And maybe he wants the Eysen. Imagine the power it might offer. You scoffed when Josh mentioned the Roswell incident back in Virginia, but are you aware that many people believed a UFO crashed in New Mexico in 1947? That the military used the new-found knowledge to advance the United States' power through technology used in everything from the moon landing, to the stealth fighters, to computers, and lots of stuff that's never even been made public?"

"Far-fetched conspiracy."

"Even if a crashed space ship never happened, the Eysen is real and the Roswell story illustrates my point. If Booker controlled the technology that created a computer this sophisti-cated, that is able to survive for millions of years . . ."

"You're right. I've been so caught up in trying to understand it and discover its secrets that I missed the bigger picture."

"Yes. If one person controlled this kind of power, he could control the world."

They sat there in silence, staring at each other and the Eysen, which circled with images of trees as if waiting for them to return their attention to the work at hand.

"So we study it in hiding, find out all there is to know, and then what? How do we go on protecting it? Sooner or later they'll find us."

Gale smiled. "They won't. They can't fight destiny. Then, when we're ready, we release it to the world. I can get the National Geographic to do it. The casing, the Eysen, and the Clastier Papers – all of it."

"And the world, ready or not, will be completely changed."

Gale nodded and quoted Clastier. "Once illuminated, it will forever alter all that is known."

END OF BOOK ONE

For a preview of COSEGA STORM (book two of the Cosega Sequence) move to the next page. Or get it now at your favorite store.

PREVIEW BOOK TWO

Cosega Storm

Tuesday July 18th

Gale and Rip sat in the courtyard surrounded by a funky desert house outside Taos, New Mexico. Gale had been trying to convince Rip that they were finally safe, but he couldn't get past his nervousness. For a week, ever since they'd run off with ancient artifacts from an archaeological dig in the mountains of Virginia, the FBI, Vatican agents, and who knew who else had been relentlessly hunting them. A trucker friendly to their cause sent them to Grinley, a drug-dealing, wacky old ex-con in whose house they now hid.

"We had a great sleep, Grinley's cooking us breakfast, and for the first time we have a whole day ahead of us to study the Eysen," Gale said.

"Okay. I'll try to relax," Rip replied.

"Good. Now, let's try to figure out how Clastier knew about the Eysen," Gale said.

Before Rip could respond, the swirl within the Eysen raced through rivers of colors. An image of a man scrawling lines onto heavy paper with a quill pen floated inside the Eysen. The bearded man, perhaps forty or fifty years old, sat at a small, pine table. Fading sunlight came into his room.

"What language is he writing in?" Miraculously, the image zoomed in closer to the page, as if responding to Gale's question.

"My God, I think it's Spanish. How could that be?" Rip asked.

"How? Wait, do you see that? *"Muchas veces nos preguntamos el verdadero valor de la vida humana. Buscamos interminables años como otros han buscado siglos de los siglos.* That's the same. I don't believe it. Rip, that's the opening to the Clastier Papers!"

Grinley's dog, Deeohjee, suddenly barked on the other side of the house, shattering the quiet morning. Something was wrong. Rip stashed the Eysen back into his pack, Gale grabbed hers, and they ran inside.

Grinley disappeared up a spiral staircase leading to the roof. Deeohjee barked out by the road and then went silent. A minute passed before Grinley slid down the railings.

"They killed my dog!" Grinley moaned. "They killed Deeohjee."

"No!" Gale cried.

"Who? Did you see anyone?" Rip asked, looking around frantically in the windowless room.

"Yeah, and it ain't the FBI," Grinley snapped. Rip thought of the Vatican agents.

"Those men out there are bloody commandos!" Grinley yelled.

"What?" Gale asked.

"They're here for us."

"They ain't here to buy weed, that's for damn sure!" Grinley pushed them around a corner and opened his gun cabinet. "Want one?"

Rip looked at Gale as Grinley pulled out several automatic rifles. "You two better not stay. Not gonna be good for any of us if you're caught here."

"How can we get out?"

Grinley grabbed a manila envelope out of the cabinet. "Follow me."

He led them into a bathroom they hadn't noticed before and pulled something inside the drain. The entire tub opened on two hydraulic tubes. Below that, he lifted a hatch. It was a short drop down to the ground. He looked up at a video monitor in the corner. There were armed figures dressed in black moving through the bushes.

"Go! There's no time."

"Where's it lead?"

"Find your way," Grinley said. "Follow it to the end. Go."

"But—" Gale started to ask.

Grinley shoved the envelope into Rip's hands along with a gun and a flashlight. At the same time, he pushed Rip down into the entrance of the tunnel. Gale slung her backpack over her shoulder and followed. Grinley closed the hatch on top of them. The tub dropped back into place, and then he headed back up to the gun turrets.

"Come on," Rip said, pulling Gale as she stared up at the dark slab they had just come from. They raced through the narrow wooden passageway until the wood ended, maybe three hundred feet into the darkness. From there the going got tough. It was a primitive tunnel, not more than two feet wide most of the time.

"Where does this go?" Gale asked, stumbling on the uneven ground.

"I don't know. It seems to be an old lava tube that someone chiseled out." Rip hit his head. "Oomph!"

"Are you okay?"

"We need to slow down a bit. It's just too narrow."

"They may already be after us. They may have killed Grinley and be on their way."

"We've got to keep moving. Grinley wouldn't have sent us if there wasn't a way out. He may be buying us time, holding them off."

Gale screamed.

Rip spun the light. She'd gone down hard. He reached to pull her up. Her wrist was bloody. "Yow," she moaned, gritting her teeth. "My leg."

"Can you walk?"

"Is there a choice?" As Gale tried to stand, a terrifying sound, inches from her head made her freeze. "Ri-p," she whispered as if it was a two-syllable word.

He turned slowly in the narrow space. "Do you need help?"

"*Snake.*"

He also froze, then heard the rattle. He moved the weak beam of his light down to her. Less than a foot from her face a large rattlesnake lay, coiled and poised to strike. Gale hardly dared to breathe. Rip thought of Grinley's gun, but there were too many reasons why that was a bad idea.

"Don't move," he said, searching for a rock. Gale didn't need to be told. He found one, not as big as he needed, but he threw it anyway. The light dropped and went dark at the same time.

Gale screamed.

"Damn," he said, trying to feel around for the flashlight.

Gale jumped up and bumped into him. He found the light. It still worked. The snake was gone. Unfortunately, they didn't know where.

"Are you okay?" he asked.

"Your rock hit me, my knee's bleeding, but the snake didn't bite me. I'm fine."

"Good, let's keep moving."

Gale limped along, heart still pounding.

"I can't believe we haven't surfaced yet," Rip said a few minutes later. "Doesn't it seem like we're going slightly downhill?"

"I was thinking the same thing."

Finally, they saw light. The tunnel ended in a small opening. Rip climbed up the rocks and peered through a space he could barely squeeze into. He gasped.

"What is it?" Gale asked.

"It's the goddamn gorge. I'm looking down a sheer cliff-maybe five or six hundred feet."

"There's no way down?"

"Not unless you can fly."

COSEGA STORM, book two of the Cosega Sequence
available at your favorite store.

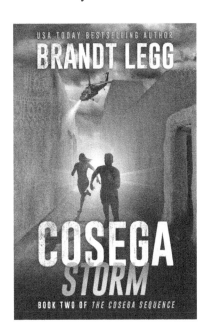

A NOTE FROM THE AUTHOR

- *Thanks for sharing the adventure*!
- **Please help** - If you enjoyed it, please post a review wherever you got the book. (even a few words). Reviews are the greatest way to help an author. And, please tell your friends.
- **I'd love to hear from you** – really. Questions, comments, whatever. Email me through my website. I'll definitely respond (within a few days).
- **Join my Inner Circle** - If you want to be the first to hear about my new releases, advance reads, occasional news and more, visit BrandtLegg.com

ABOUT THE AUTHOR

USA TODAY Bestselling Author Brandt Legg uses his unusual real life experiences to create page-turning novels. He's traveled with CIA agents, dined with senators and congressmen, mingled with astronauts, chatted with governors and presidential candidates, had a private conversation with a Secretary of Defense he still doesn't like to talk about, hung out with Oscar and Grammy winners, had drinks at the State Department, been pursued by tabloid reporters, and spent a birthday at the White House by invitation from the President of the United States.

At age eight, Legg's father died suddenly, plunging his family into poverty. Two years later, while suffering from crippling migraines, he started in business, and turned a hobby into a multi-million-dollar empire. National media dubbed him the "Teen Tycoon," and by the mid-eighties, Legg was one of the top young entrepreneurs in America, appearing as high as number twenty-four on the list (when Steve Jobs was #1, Bill Gates #4, and Michael Dell #6). Legg still jokes that he should have gone into computers.

By his twenties, after years of buying and selling businesses, leveraging, and risk-taking, the high-flying Legg became ensnarled in the financial whirlwind of the junk bond eighties. The stock market crashed and a firestorm of trouble came down. The Teen Tycoon racked up more than a million dollars in legal fees, was betrayed by those closest to him, lost his entire fortune, and ended up serving time for financial improprieties.

After a year, Legg emerged from federal prison, chastened and wiser, and began anew. More than twenty-five years later, he's now using all that hard-earned firsthand knowledge of conspiracies, corruption and high finance to weave his tales. Legg's books pulse with authenticity.

His series have excited nearly a million readers around the world. Although he refused an offer to make a television movie about his life as a teenage millionaire, his autobiography is in the works. There has also been interest from Hollywood to turn his thrillers into films. With any luck, one day you'll see your favorite characters on screen.

He lives in the Pacific Northwest, with his wife and son, writing full time, in several genres, containing the common themes of adventure, conspiracy, and thrillers. Of all his pursuits, being an author and crafting plots for novels is his favorite.

For more information, please visit his website, or to contact Brandt directly, email him: Brandt@BrandtLegg.com, he loves to hear from readers and always responds!

BrandtLegg.com

BOOKS BY BRANDT LEGG

CapWar ELECTION (CapStone Conspiracy #1)

CapWar EXPERIENCE (CapStone Conspiracy #2)

CapWar EMPIRE (CapStone Conspiracy #3)

Cosega Search (Cosega Sequence #1)

Cosega Storm (Cosega Sequence #2)

Cosega Shift (Cosega Sequence #3)

Cosega Sphere (Cosega Sequence #4)

The Last Librarian (Justar Journal #1)

The Lost TreeRunner (Justar Journal #2)

The List Keepers (Justar Journal #3)

Outview (Inner Movement #1)

Outin (Inner Movement #2)

Outmove (Inner Movement #3)

ACKNOWLEDGMENTS

I began work on Cosega Search after waking up with the basic plot in my head back in the 90s. It was my first attempt at writing fiction. However, real life quickly got in the way and my dream of being an author was shelved. By the time I arranged things so I could finally finish a novel, twenty years had elapsed, and another story – the Inner Movement – was pressing for attention. Cosega had to wait once more. Very little of what I wrote so long ago remains in this final work, but the core story is the same. I believe what became the Cosega Sequence is much better now due to the two decades it took to get this story out.

There are many who helped; Roanne Legg, Barbara Blair, Harriet Greene, and Marty Goldman, who read early drafts and offered invaluable input. Bonnie Brown Koeln made every accommodation to meet the deadlines, including reading while traveling. And Elizabeth Chumney, who returned from the past to do the final read. A special thanks to Mike Sager for publishing my first trilogy. And finally to Teakki, who patiently waited, and built with Legos, until I finished writing each day.

Made in the USA
Monee, IL
30 September 2021